The Sunlit Clearing

The Sunlit Clearing

Stories

Bruce Adam

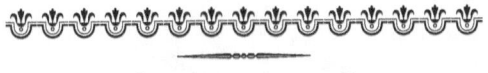

☙ Ara Pacis ❧

The Sunlit Clearing, Stories, Volume 5

First Edition, 2015

Ara Pacis Publishers
P.O. Box 1202
Des Plaines, IL 60017-1202
www.arapacispublishers.com

ISBN-10: 0-9821277-9-0
ISBN-13: 978-0-9821277-9-7

Library of Congress Control Number: 2014921494

Manufactured in the United States of America.

Contents

To my friend Ford Russell

The Sunlit Clearing

...the huge jungle of the unconscious mind, of which the conscious mind is merely a sunlit clearing.

~ Anthony Burgess

The Warehouse

I'm in an expansive warehouse in which I discover many strange things, most of which I recognize in a strange sort of way. It is like I wandered out of a dream into this place as if it were a storage room for my dreams, except obviously everything is broken here. I find the heads of people I used to know and plenty of headless bodies, and I can see all the pieces are interchangeable. It occurs to me that perhaps this is the assembly room of my dreams.

I see my family pretty well accounted for and torn apart in various phases of their lives: my mother at various ages, my father as a boy and as a man, but all versions ripped apart. I also find pieces of my old house, the front door, the piece of a wall in my room next to my bed with the drawings on it, and this too is torn in half, more ripped like a brick went through it, though it is something I've thought about many times in ways where I would think if I had a chance to possess it that I would want it intact.

Other things look like they were hit with an axe. There are things from my old schools, chalkboards including one with the math problem I could only half finish to the delight of the teacher who teased me until I sat down crying. There's also all my baseball equipment, my mitt and spikes, not aged and used up like they really were when my parents refused to replace them, but in brand new condition, not yet ripped apart and unusable.

It is dark in the warehouse, but there is a soft flickering light from windows up high that allows me to see in this place. Also, from beyond the windows where the light is, I can hear muted noises that sound familiar as I focus on them, voices of people I knew, and a familiar car engine with the old knocking.

Then I find a door that leads me into a new area, and as I enter, the sounds increase substantially in volume and intensity so I know whatever is generating them is close. There is fear here, and even panic. I hear crying and screaming. I also hear my parents fighting, yet fearing for their lives. The only light is coming from a barrel that I can feel is fueled by all my old dance steps from high school. I don't know how I know this, but I'm certain by the way they're burning that it's filled with the dances I never danced because I was always afraid to dance. It's the only way to explain the extent of the flames, and there are plenty more to fuel the raging fire.

Then I see a silhouette against a far wall, cast there by the light from the burning barrel. It is making a chopping motion, swinging something. I sneak over and see it is myself. I have an axe and am slashing through people and things I have lived. It is me, obviously livid and crazed, a wrecking ball of sorts, filling the warehouse of my mind with the mulch of my days. I fear that he will see me and come after me, unsure whether he will attack or ask for my assistance. Afraid either way, I cringe and hide there, up to my neck in pieces of my broken past.

The Snow Job

A violent and lengthy snowstorm has blanketed the earth in two miles of snow, but within days emergency crews have dug out tunnels, and soon I am able to drive to work, to the store, and just about anywhere I need to go. I am amazed at how well everyone responded to the disaster! Sure, there are two miles of snow above us, but in some ways it is like nothing has happened. Lights have been put in with dimmers so daylight can be simulated. It is all very nice, and I am happy in this winter wonderland.

Then I hear that there is a plan to dump the snow on a neighboring country or state, which has not been decided, but clearly where the people would not be equipped to deal with it. Millions would suffer and die. I am about to complain but I see water droplets are starting to fall. Then I hear the weather has changed, and it is all turning to slush and that we will be the ones to suffer and die after all, but the closer it comes to that, I find myself relieved to hear there is still an ongoing, desperate push to dump it on others, even though I fear it is too late.

The Vacant Husband

I no longer trust my wife as there have been numerous situations of an ambiguous nature suggesting that she is having an affair, and I am now determined to find out for myself whether she is cheating on me. The house across the street is abandoned, and I break into it to make it my headquarters for the operation of seeing whether she brings anyone home while I'm supposedly away on a business trip.

To complicate matters, a divorced woman who lives on the next street behind the abandoned house sees me climbing through the back window one evening and demands to know what I am doing. I lie and convince her that I am on a police stakeout, and she becomes very excited and enthusiastic. She keeps a watchful eye on me from her house, and brings me coffee and sandwiches through the night. One thing leads to another, and soon we are having an affair in the abandoned house, which she begins to decorate and make more comfortable, at least as far as the bedroom is concerned.

At no time during my covert operation do I detect that my wife is cheating, but I must confess I'm not keeping a very close watch. Then this woman tells me a story about the abandoned house we're in, that it was once occupied by a happy couple, but the husband used to slip out at night and have a cigarette by the back gate, where he saw a pretty neighbor through a kitchen window, which was the woman telling me the story. She explains that she herself blew the whistle on the whole affair when he tried to break it off and go back to his wife, so being with a man in this bedroom has a certain poignancy attached to it.

I do not see the sentimental value of being in a home she wrecked, but I honestly have no intentions of divorcing my wife now that I know I can trust her. I tell the woman that my stakeout could end at any time, and I might not show up on a given night, but that whatever happens I will be in touch.

Before she leaves toward morning, she kisses me, and gathering up all my things, I clear out and drive into the city where I wait until evening and come home from my "business trip" to see my wife and kids for the first time in a couple of weeks. I feel a great mixture of conflicting emotions. On the one hand, I am glad in that I have come to the conclusion that my wife is not cheating on me, and as I hug her, I try to convey an extra burst of love. But there is a break in the cement that holds the reservoir of marital trust, which I can feel has all but drained away and that I have to completely fake the moment. I am just a husk of my former self.

Cutting Both Ways

I look in the mirror and realize that my head is a double-edged sword. Not only that, as soon as I walk outside, I am attacked like a minnow in open waters. Somehow I find I am able to thwart the attackers by swinging my head to one side, only one side, and soon I am victorious.

Later I realize that I am able to use the other side of the sword for peaceful purposes such as cutting bread and fish, or creating furrows in the ground for planting seed. I am a great help to the people in the village, but one day I make a mistake and use the wrong edge. I hurt the mayor who calls in the enemy and tells them my weakness. And so they attack me from the other side, wave after wave of them. I prepare them fish sandwiches to no avail. I prepare furrows for the planting of seed all for naught.

It seems wounding a friend by accident is worse than helping enemies on purpose. I am terrified to see a giant sheath coming my way, shaped like me and something into which I will fit that will come to permanent rest on a concrete slab. I recognize it as my end in sight.

Episode

I come home, and my wife and children are gone. Another woman has taken up residence, and she hugs me when I come through the door. She speaks, but I do not understand anything she says. I point to the door, expecting her to realize that I want her to leave, but instead she grabs a cloth and starts cleaning it. I tell her that I want her to go, and she begins cleaning the floor. Nothing I do can get rid of her, so I decide the best thing to do is wait and keep my distance.

But as I go through the house, I see that she has already begun to erase all the signs that I ever had a wife and family. My daughter's room no longer has the plastic bubbles on the wall. Her polkadot bedspread is gone as are all of the stuffed animals and posters that she treasured.

My oldest son's room has also been completely redecorated. Even the smell of his cologne is gone, and though I never much cared for the scent, I really miss it now.

My youngest son's room is also totally revamped. It's again set up like a business office and reminds me of the one I used to have before any of the children were born. I used to sit there at the desk and look out the window at the pine tree and reflect on my future. What would it bring?

Now everything is gone except this strange woman. But when I go into my own bedroom, it is all the same, and all of my wife's' things are still in place. It is then that I realize the woman is my wife and that our children have all grown up and have moved out. They now have lives of their own, and I am just having another one of my "episodes."

Decoding

I have worked many years to create the perfect illusion of myself, and I have only succeeded by burying all of my secrets, putting them out of the way by a coded adjustment of their reality, meaning that even though they may be present, no one can see them but me, for only I know the combination, the way they are turned slightly out of phase with reality to be just beyond view and completely out of reach to everyone. And so I live in this pristine environment, with not a single element out of place, no whiff of scandal or controversy of any kind because, as I said, every bit of it is properly hidden, so perfectly concealed it would be impossible for anyone to discover even a single one of them even by some kind of accident.

It is unimaginable even if someone might for some reason be suspicious and go looking for something, which of course they are not. Everyone is totally comfortable with me, and I only receive respect in every way from all. But suddenly that all changes in an instant with a kind of earthquake that hits my life. I'd be more inclined to call it a "symmetrical incident," for it seems it came about by a chance that I may have stumbled on a degree of order that is itself hidden. When I went to hide one more thing and put in a code, it must have aligned with all the other codes and set them in motion to reveal them all at once, and once and for all.

My walls, floors and ceilings are now inscribed with every terrible thing I have done. It is as if some brilliant sculptor has come to put it all in relief. It bulges out and stares at me and everyone else who comes to see me, only they don't come now. It is a great shame, inside and outside my house, so perfectly carved, all of it in high relief.

Slime

I am a slug. I am alert to this fact and disturbed by it, but I don't know if I should inform the other slugs about my discontent. There are millions of us, and we have finally inherited the world, which we are handling as well as one might expect for a bunch of slugs. I remember when I was a child, and my father used to say that there was a natural progression of the generations, that there was a rise and fall. He explained that back when the nation first formed, the original generation was very independent and steadfast, faithful and able to endure hardships without losing hope or nerve.

I heard about the war that he fought, and I recalled the message of the best films of his generation. It was always the individual spirit at odds with corrupt powers, and in the end, his spirit is not only victorious, but he also gets the girl.

But after fighting that war, they raised us, we thought, without giving us room to breathe. We needed to push the envelope, and without any real and refined sense of justice, we descended on and questioned every law that we could. By degrees we changed it all, and now the movies are shockers of murderous mayhem with no moral backbone or message.

Now it is possible for a man to marry a donkey or a dog, and why not! All over the globe, the rest of the slugs are just like the slugs over here. We are all for ourselves and for having what we want, whatever it is, without any consideration of the consequences, so we fish the oceans dry, build walls to block the salmon runs, cut down forests, et cetera; and of course, we declared it's wrong, but we don't do anything about it, for we wouldn't be slugs if we did. We do know how to correct children who bring plastic knives to school, just as our children know how to shoot their classmates en masse.

I'm sorry, but as a slug I am slow to respond. I have just been leaving a trail of slime on a newspaper I've been sliding slowly across at my own pace, and I tend to project a little of what I read as I go along. Now that I'm off the paper and back on grass, I'm feeling much, much better.

The Demon

I have a meeting with my demon with whom I arranged the sale of my soul many years ago, and I express my growing dissatisfaction with the way things have turned out in my life. What began as a manifestation of a gift that thrilled and delighted my wife and family, slowly led to degrees of greater and greater separation from them which resulted in an ever-lessening affection that completely vanished over many years.

The demon is hard-pressed to understand why I am complaining when he has delivered everything that was promised in our arrangement. He says he held up his side of the bargain, that my work is of the highest quality. It is unique and interesting.

But even I know that is true, yet in another sense, I alone know it. Nobody else seems interested anymore. It is as if these people wanted something else out of me, like love and happiness, but in keeping my part with the demon, those goals were miraculously and meticulously pruned so that I did not deliver these most basic elements of life. Without the love, kindness and concern that they wanted, they were not interested anymore in my craft, even though it was now of the highest order.

And now my TV dinners are coming dry and cold. The meat is left over from another day. Nobody sits with me at the table. I sense that I should be saying and doing things to court them, but I have grown cold and dry myself. My loved ones all have long faces when I am around. I have slowly brought them down to this level, slowly separated myself from them.

But now I realize that what I have given up for my goals was more fulfilling than the work itself, and even I don't care anymore about all I've accomplished. I care for it about as little as anyone cares about me.

The Spirit

There is a great wind, an explosion, an earthquake and the power goes out, and the sudden combination of all these things removes a spirit from me. I see it come out of me and hover just beyond me, out of reach, affected by the wind and unable to get back inside me.

With its release, I feel an immediate sense of who I was many years before. It is like I am myself again, something I have not known in a long time and now wish to preserve at all costs, for I know this to be the spirit of fear that has left me, and I wonder how it managed to take hold of me for so long and why I didn't do anything about it.

I decide to ask it this question, and it doesn't respond. I assume that it entered me through other people with whom I spent a great deal of time. I remember that indeed I had acquired some of the behaviors of people I'd lived with. It was as though through them I would learn to behave in ways I did not like. Now I realize I had let this thing into my life by degrees. I must not have known it was there at the beginning when it mattered most, when it would be most easily recognized against the backdrop of my normal self and be most easily removed.

Then I hear someone come in behind me, but I cannot turn to look. I am frozen somehow. I cannot move. Now I see a group of people in front of me. They are firemen and policemen who have come to investigate the explosion that killed me. Now I look up at the spirit and realize it isn't simply the spirit of fear. It is my very life itself. I call it back, but it dissipates and drifts away, and I am put into a black bag, and into total darkness as it is zipped shut.

Appearances

One of my friends is telling me that he no longer wishes to see a woman, and then she walks in and interrupts our conversation. Now that I see her and know how he feels, I feel sorry for her. When she leaves, I do everything I can to convince him to give it another try, stressing the importance of forgiveness and acceptance as keys to a good relationship.

But he explains that she has let her hair grow on parts of her body that men expect women to shave, and I tell him that she is from another country, and if she stays here long enough, she will adapt the ways of women here.

Then he tells me other things, each more difficult to explain away, until I myself am so disgusted that I wonder how he went so long with a woman who had so many bad habits and disgusting ways about her.

She enters the room again, and as the light from the window washes over her, I suddenly see she has enormous beauty under all that body hair, and I suddenly want to be with her. I approach her later when she is alone. She is crying that my friend has rejected her, but she is repelled by me. I ask her why, and she explains that my friend has told her terrible things about me, and when she entered the room, and the light washed over me, she saw that everything he said about me was true, that there is an awful ugliness beneath my good looks.

Pawns

I am on a chessboard, and I realize that the other pieces are my friends. Suddenly they begin falling over one by one even though no moves have been made to take them out of the game. I cannot leave my square to help anyone, but I can see the kind of distress they are in as they lie in crumpled heaps where they once stood proudly. Despite the sudden change in their appearance, the game continues with no consideration for their condition, and this surprises me as very few of them would be considered pawns.

The chess pieces themselves are all based on automobiles, so perhaps it isn't readily noticed that the drivers inside are in distress. Also larger hands are manipulating the pieces, so their driving skills aren't really required. I happen to be the king on my side of the board, and I have tiny magnetic replicas of the holy family on my dashboard. As the game progresses, these holy replicas begin to seem to experience some physical distress as well. Their color begins to bleach out as if they were getting too much sun, and the lack of water has them standing with tongues out, looking delirious.

Only Christ Himself continues to stand tall, unaffected by forty days of driving in the desert. But despite His power to heal, He does nothing for the now doubled over magnetic figures of the friends and family around him. I guess He knows what He is doing, that there is a larger game plan at stake.

Now I realize I have taken my eye off the game and what it is going to cost me. By concentrating my attention on the holy figurines, all of my friends and family are in major distress or gone. I now can see we are at a disadvantage in the game. I am all alone except for a few pieces now, quite out of commission though they continue to serve as best they can. Such is the nobility of human nature. As the end nears, I do everything I can to relax, but even so, I can feel myself twisting and contorting, turning into some kind of pretzel. I can see Christ waving on the dashboard. I assume He's doing all He can for me, and then I notice we are in the car crusher, quickly becoming encased in a cube as the game ends, and He is asking me to save Him.

I see no problem with that, and so I lift him off my dash and throw him out into the window of the shiny new white Chevy idling nearby, ready for the next game. He lands and attaches to the dashboard, and the traffic light turns green.

Counting Time

After all my years of fierce living and scrambling, I am scratched over with many small scars, some larger ones in there as well, but one wouldn't actually know most of them were scars and might rather mistake them for wrinkles, and a wrinkle specialist might want to bring me back from a road trip to stand before his boss as a living example to prove his wrinkle report is accurate because it's ridiculous how many of those I have as well. But I received both my wrinkles and scars for years of service, and my reward is a stainless steel watch with a sapphire crystal that will not scratch.

I had to put on my glasses to see the small numbers on the various smaller totalizers on the dial of the watch, to see that these are for measuring the moon phases, the months and even the years ahead, though I do not have too many of those left. I really can't even tell the time on the thing without my glasses, and quite frankly I've learned by experience to generally know what time it is at any given time of day by the quality of light outside or just by how I feel at a given moment.

I feel this is as hard and good a watch as anyone could ever want to measure time, but I have become a pretty good measurer of time myself for having lived so much of it, and to give me something so clean, precise and scratch resistant when I am so much the opposite seems somehow inappropriate. Did they ever take the time to know me? How is it that we can differentiate a person from a tree at a great distance, but we avoid discovering what they are behind the eyes? It is as if we believe the information is written too small for our weak eyes to read, and rather than even squinting and making the attempt, we draw general conclusions and make harsh judgements on the scantiest information as if we had the inner ability to know the nature of another's soul from having been immersed in life with one ourselves.

So I don't even want the watch, and I give it to my grandson, who's too young to use it and only a short time away from putting it in his drawer, and he says, "Grandpa, did you see yourself here like Mickey Mouse? It's you on the watch." And I don't even have to look. I can feel it already all over, and I can see myself tied down on a dial being used as some kind of a measurer of moon phases, for hours, days, weeks, months and years; and I can also see how I have so many wrinkles from the sun, but the scars I did to myself from everyday use, something referred to as general wear and tear.

Now I understand why my arms are so sore, why I'm so tired of everything, and why I feel like I'm always looking through a window and always know what time it is, and given how the kids look at me with all their gadgets with built-in clocks but nothing traditional like a wristwatch, I'm feeling pretty obsolete.

The Defense Attorney

I am a lawyer who has defended people who happen to do things that some people find sinful and nauseating, so much so that someone would go so far as to kill these people, and sadly there has been a history of that. But the point I make rather well is that these people are adults and all are only doing such things in their private lives as adults. Therefore there should be more tolerance and flexibility in society for these people since in many ways we are the same in that we would not wish to have our private lives opened and scrutinized as it would be very likely that something would be found distasteful to those judging us. Thus I always conclude that we should live and let live and not be so hasty to judge others.

I must say with great satisfaction that my efforts to defend these people have been successful as my cases have established precedence in many areas, and not only are there new laws protecting my clients, but there have been major advances in allowance for their interests, meaning that they can in many ways speak openly and publicly of what they do without fear of ignorant reprisal.

But when I come home from court, I am appalled to learn that my seven-year-old son has been learning about some of these adult choices in class. He is being taught that such things are normal and main stream. The teachers are reading books that offer these ideas as alternative lifestyles, which astonishes me since they have always been regarded as aberrations concealed at the adult level, and even though the laws have changed, they are still private matters between consenting adults, not appropriate subject matter for children's books aimed at primary school children.

But when I raise this question, I immediately am shouted down in the hallways by new associates of a new mindset. As new steps are taken to indoctrinate my son, a new process is underway to have me disbarred.

Sweat Lodge

I am in attendance at an Indian ritual that is taking place in a sweat lodge, an oblong hut in the desert, inside which there is a fire, many rocks, a spiritual leader and many people like myself looking for spiritual guidance and fulfillment. The rocks have been selected for their marvelous drawings, which I find fascinating. These were prepared by artisans in trances in sweat lodges like this one in ages past.

The entire hut is built of these rocks, and so they are visible all around me, not just near the fire but in the walls. At intervals, the spiritual leader begins to pour water on the stones, and the steam rises and fills the room. I am soon feeling very hot, too hot for comfort, and though I wish to leave the hut, I cannot. My only solace is to observe the engravings on the rocks and try to lose myself in reflecting on the designs. By doing this, I feel myself among spirits with whom I am exchanging soul maps, by which we give our all without losing anything, and we receive ever so much in return because the soul is mapped completely and retained in such a way that it lives within the one who receives it. So now I contain many souls.

All at once I hear shrieking because some of the rocks are cracking as the water hits them. The spiritual leader curses. He is evidently a fraud. These turn out to be river rocks with air pockets. They could explode at any moment. The drawings are not ancient. They are faked, or perhaps copied from genuine rocks. This is just a sweat lodge mill, designed to bilk people out of their hard-earned cash.

Soon the rocks do begin exploding. A huge shard hits me on the chest, and the heat tattoos the design on me. Another rock explodes and does the same thing, searing the reverse image of a carving on another part of me. Mayhem ensues. Rocks explode all around like a fireworks finale, and by the end of it, I am covered with these ritualistic designs.

Then the dome collapses, and I alone survive. I find my way to a village and am nursed back to health by people mesmerized by my body art. They see me as a having been sent to them as an act of heavenly intervention. I am revered as a spiritual leader, and in a real sweat lodge with real rocks that can't explode, I am installed as their spiritual leader, a job and title I feel I've earned.

Rejuvenation

I am an old man nearing the end of my days, and I'm walking in the woods, when it suddenly grows very dark and begins to rain. I can see a big storm is coming so I try to hurry, but I am old and don't move well. Drenching rain begins to fall, and many flashes of lightning fill the woods with light. Great deafening peals of thunder follow and resonate around me.

Suddenly lightning strikes a tree near me, causing it to fall toward me. I cannot get out of the way fast enough, and it lands right on top of me. But I find myself sitting on top of the tree, not underneath it, and I feel great. I am able to run, and I speed through the woods and return home.

Once inside, I go immediately to the bathroom to remove my wet clothes and dry off. I happen to look in the mirror, and I'm shocked to see that I am a very young man again. I see a doctor who confirms that I am in perfect health and about 25 years old.

I am thrilled, overwhelmed! I have a great deal of money in the bank from a lifetime of working and saving, and I begin to live it up, to enjoy myself as I never have before. It is as if now that I have a new life, I have a new attitude about how to live it. I go out on the town. I live like there is no tomorrow. I make many contacts with people, but none of them are important to me, and all the relationships are superficial. I watched all my friends die in my other life, and I do not want to do anything, or come to know anyone such that I care for them and have to suffer again to watch new friends die later.

I go on like this for years. Then someone who tries to get to know me says that I am dead inside and asks me if I might already have died. I laugh it off but I do not like hearing that I have no soul just because I seek gratification in the moment and have no other goals but to find pleasure.

But I continue to think about it until finally something makes me go back to the forest to the place where the tree fell. I rent a piece of heavy machinery to move the tree, and when I push it to the side, I discover that my old bones are indeed there and that I have been killed. Nothing tastes good or feels good after that.

Decay

I am letting a tooth go. I noticed it had a hole in it, feeling it with my tongue, and I could see it in the mirror, but I decided not to do anything about it. I just said to myself, "Let it go." So I decided not to do anything about it. I just don't care.

When I was young, my parents always taught me to take care of problems when they start, but I don't care about this tooth. I plan to just let it go. I think, "What does it matter anyway, at my age? I will turn to dust anyway. Nobody's looking in my mouth, and as long as it's been since I've been to a dentist, I don't want to hear any lectures about how I should be taking better care of myself."

But I think this is no ordinary tooth. The cavity has been growing for a while, but I feel no pain. If anything, this tooth comes equipped with its own anesthetic, numbing me as it decays. The longer the tooth is decaying, the longer I let it go, the better I feel about it, the more I think it's the right thing to do, the more I believe I have the right attitude.

I wouldn't be surprised if the hole went all the way into my jaw. Moreover, I wouldn't be surprised if it went further than that. I honestly believe this hole goes straight to my heart and soul, or if it's not there yet, it's getting close. I'm beginning to feel numb there as well, and I've stopped brushing and have started eating candy to speed it up. I want to feel numb in my heart and soul, as numb as can be.

Anticipation

I can see myself as a little boy sitting up in bed looking out the window of my bedroom, mostly listening or trying to hear the music in the distance, which I knew to be coming from an evening concert at the public pool. I wanted to go, but I was not old enough. It was for people a few years older than me, and I remember feeling this way a lot when I was a boy, that there were always people in front of me able to do more than I could, and I resented it. I wanted to be older and move up in line, closer to the front. I wanted to be allowed to do things, to go places, and in time, my turn arrived.

It arrived with a vengeance. But I still find myself in line after all these years. I find myself behind people only a little older than me, and again there is a huge difference, only now it is manifested in ability, in mental capacity, in wrinkles, and in strength. I know I will move up quickly in line for how quickly I have reached the point where I am, but as I stand here, waiting my turn for dinner, I look back to that night in my bed when I craned my neck and put my ear to the screen to hear the music.

I remember how the wind played with the sound. It seemed to blow it one way, prevented it from reaching my ears, then allowed it passage where I could enjoy the sounds for a few moments.

Now I am standing where I'd looked to be only a few years back, and those ahead of me by only a few years aren't looking so good. As a boy, everyone a few years ahead of me could stay up later. These people a few years ahead of me need to go to sleep earlier now. The kids ahead of me were more robust and could run faster and jump higher than me. These people ahead of me now can neither run nor jump without injuring themselves.

It is quiet in the room. No one is speaking. All at once, I hear the same song that was played at the public pool years ago. Someone has turned on a radio. I crane my neck to hear it, but it is so low, it comes and goes like it's caught in the wind. Then someone a few years older than me with more seniority in the nursing home orders the music turned down, and I remember my hearing isn't what it used to be. That night I sit on my bed in front of the window, and I hear sirens going to one emergency or another. The wind plays tricks with them. From time to time, it sounds like they're coming straight for me as I know they will someday, but then in the next moment, they are just background noises again, drowned out by the song in my heart.

Gems

I live in a world where men are made of stone and diamonds take the place of hearts. Without such a gem inside, new life cannot exist, so all of life is bound up in searching for diamonds so that the population can be expanded. This is a governmental edict. Everyone works in the mines, and everyone is expendable because life is so important. Once diamonds are found, they are quickly taken away by agents of the government, after which the rubble where they were found is trucked away. Usually in this rubble are the remnants of some very good stone men who were destroyed in order to retrieve the diamonds, the ones inside them, to meet that day's quota. It is common practice to place a couple of sticks of dynamite in the rear crevices of an unsuspecting victim and blow him up. It also opens up a new area for digging. Several times I have heard a hiss behind me and have removed dynamite from my back just in time. It is very dangerous work to say the least. We never really know whether the diamonds we mine are put to good use to increase the population or to build an army. My wife and I want a family and have applied for a diamond, but so far we have been denied, as has everyone else, it seems. I don't know anyone who has been granted one, but the managers say it goes mine to mine, and we hear stories that in other places everyone has kids. One day while I'm working, I see a stone man I don't recognize crawling over a rock pile. I ask him what he's doing here, and he says he came a long way because he heard we all have children here. I tell him it's not true. Later, I see he has been detained, and I watch as they blow him up to retrieve his diamond, and I think, to silence him. I do not tell my wife about this. She is desperate and wants me to get a diamond at any price so we can make a child with one. To create new life, I have to take a life. There is an old stone man who I think would make an easy target. I'm often alone with him in inner areas of the mine, and I know he trusts me, but as strange as it may sound, what's holding me back is that I actually feel less aversion to the idea of killing an old friend than to bringing a new child into this awful place.

The Journey

My friend Jimmer and I are almost ready to come home with our families after a long and successful accumulation of stuff in a distant land. Our final items are two white boats that require a nod from a corrupt official if we are going to obtain them. There is a payoff necessary, but given the region, there's no guarantee we will get the boats even with the bribe. We're a bit worried about that as well as bringing everything home where our story will be that we received the boats as a gift. The corrupt official is supposed to provide papers to that effect, which will cut down on duties enormously.

When we finally meet with the official, he asks Jimmer in a menacing tone, "Where did you get these boats?"

"As a gift," Jimmer replies.

"Papers please!" shouts the official.

"But you have them, sir," Jimmer stammers back.

"Ah, so I do. Everything is in order," laughs the official, and he hands the papers over and gives me a look like, "Get out of here before I change my mind," and it is clear the situation can change, fall through at any moment. So we leave in haste with the boats in tow and hand them over to some associates who will stow them on the ship, and then we make our way to the river, which we have to cross in order to get to the ship.

As soon as we reach the water, Jimmer seems confused about how to cross, and he tries to lead me into the water, walking in the muddy water up to his knees. I stand on the shore and ask what the heck he's trying to do. I say that it's not like we still have the boats, but I know he's still nervous from dealing with bribing the official, and I understand it given who he is as I've seen similar behavior in the past. Once when we were teenagers and he was visiting, the police were chasing us through a field familiar to me but not to Jimmer, so I told him to stay close to me, but he panicked and veered away to take a different course, got lost, and doubled back right into the hands of the authorities. Since then, I've never forgotten this weakness or propensity of his to lose his cool in tough situations. On the other hand, he was always very athletic and as long as there were no sudden surprises, he has used his abilities to help get us through some tough situations. But once he perceives a problem he locks in to whatever course he's on and can't be dissuaded.

So I stand at the river for a while, waiting for him to realize that we don't have to ford the river because just down the way, there's a bridge that goes across directly to the ship. Jimmer appeals to me to come with him, that everything will be OK, but I continue to refuse, hoping his brain will unfreeze on the issue. I point to the bridge and ask him to look at the possibility of going that way, and gradually, he begins to snap out of it. Finally he comes out of the water, and I lead him to the bridge where we cross over to the ship where I see the bags and luggage being loaded. We're set to depart in just a few hours.

Once on board, we make our way to our berth. Jimmer complains about his wet pants, but I keep telling him he can change soon. The situation with the official still seems to be bothering him because even before we climb up into the berth, I notice he is trying to take off his pants. I lose my patience and yell at him to wait a few minutes, and this has the effect of making him more nervous. I pat him on the back and say that everything will be alright, not to worry, that I'll go up and get him his pants, and then I tried to climb up to the berth ahead of him, but he pushed me away and went up ahead of me with the same look on his face as when he took his own path while we were running across the field.

As I come up to the top of the ladder behind him, I notice that he came earlier and packed his area with items beyond the weight limit. There are things he shouldn't even be taking like the several large, flat stones indigenous to the area, quite interesting, but we had agreed earlier that we would not be taking such things with us. He stacked these on the third shelf toward the bottom, and there is so much stuff filling the berth that Jimmer has to put his feet on the shelf next to the rocks. His added weight causes the shelf to shift down and the rocks to slide toward him. Seeing what's about to happen, I yell at Jimmer to watch out. Just in time, he jumps, and they slide against the wall with a crash. A millisecond later, Jimmer lands on top of them.

"Good jump," I say.

"Yes, it was, wasn't it?" he replies, but it is obvious that the jump has thrown out his back. I can see he's in distress trying to deal with the spasms, and he looks for a place to sit down, but with all the stuff everywhere, the only place he can sit down is on the rocks beneath his feet. So rather gingerly he takes his time and sits down, sliding a bit down the wall of the berth into which the stones have crashed, and the combined weight of the stones pressing there with his full weight coming down to a seated position pushes out the wall so that the rocks slide further as the wall buckles. Suddenly the floor of the berth collapses, and I watch in horror as Jimmer, the rocks and the rest of his stuff, crashes down to the concourse beneath us. From where I'm standing, I don't have a full view through the opening in the floor, but from the sound of the crash and the distance he fell, not to mention all the stuff that followed him down, I can only surmise that he is either terribly injured or has been killed in the fall. I call down to him but hear nothing except the commotion of an emergency response below. Through the crack I see the authorities have arrived, and somehow, despite the tragic nature of the moment, I feel a certain calm fatality that this is exactly the way it was always meant to end for him.

Parasites

I enter a machine that is designed to recognize and isolate one's temptations as the tentacles grow inside, then in a strange and miraculous way, remove them from the inside and place them on the outside of the body where they can be clearly seen in all their parasitic ugliness, then dealt with. I wonder why the word "removed" is not used in the description. What does it mean, "dealt with?" But I am beset with so many temptations that they have taken over within me. I am their slave. So I have come to this machine not just in the hope of change, but to save my life. It feels like the last chance I have, and I am desperate to do anything.

So I enter the machine, and the operator throws the switch. Immediately I feel very strange sensations. The slithering I felt inside, all the itching of desire, feels relieved for a moment, and suddenly I feel like scratching myself all over the outside as I am itchy everywhere. The treatment complete, the door opens, and I exit the machine, and in a mirror I see what looks like hundreds of tentacles of an octopus growing out of me, winding their way around me. The operator gives me clippers and tells me I must cut them off, one by one. But when I try to clip one off, I feel terrible pain. He tells me to hurry before they consume me. Already they are bigger, and I hardly have any strength to lift the shears, let alone use them to cut the tentacles. Instinctively, I seek relief in the ocean water, where the tentacles devour what is left of me before splitting off to grow and breed as individuals.

Thinking Straight

I'm in a universe where everything is curved, and I make the mistake of saying, "Let me get this straight," to someone who mistakenly surmises from my casual statement that I have some kind of psychotic tendencies and terrorist intentions or agenda to destroy the universe by taking the natural bend out of everything. So I am arrested based on his accusations and brought before a government tribunal, which quickly finds me guilty and throws me in prison.

There I meet others who have been treated in much the same way, normal people like myself who do not abide by strict bureaucratic rules, and we form a secret society whose aim it is to change the world. In this group, it is my job to create a formula for straightening the universe should our subterfuge be detected. We agree that we would only employ it as a last resort, or to hold it up as a threat unless our demands are met, but the point is moot without a formula.

So there's a lot of pressure on me, and working hard over the next several months, I finally isolate a formula for straightening out a single part of the universe that will result in a chain reaction and straighten out everything, but it is so simple that I fear telling anyone about it. When asked, I just say that I am still working on it.

Given I have this formula like a hot potato in my pocket, it's all I think about, and my thoughts are all over the place. I begin to wonder whether we would all be better off if the universe were straightened out. Perhaps it would do better starting over, and over billions of years, life would form somewhere that wouldn't even compare to our sorry state, it would be so perfect. I might be doing the universe a big favor. But who knows, maybe it would be worse off in some subtle way. The differences might not be so obvious given that some curves are so slight one thinks things seem straight over long distances. Suffice it to say, all of this thinking has my head spinning in its normal curves, and I wish I could straighten out my thinking without it affecting the rest of the universe.

But it is all up to me whether I start the chain reaction. I know if I say I would do it and hold up the formula as a threat without revealing it, nobody would believe me. They would think it was a bluff. I do have the power, but taking action is something I must either do or not do without telling anyone. I wish I could forget about it entirely, just go back to the way it was, but being in prison for making a silly comment gives me reason enough that this revolutionary plan should sit in the forefront of my mind. I deserve to have my revenge, but it is a big step to be the father of a complete makeover for everyone, to end life as everyone knows it, and I'm not sure I'm ready to take on that responsibility. Given I can't even be sure what the end result would be, a chain reaction of confusion begins to take over my brain and ravages it with such force that my mind is quickly tied up in knots that cannot be undone.

Floods

I'm in some kind of fortress which is more like a maze. It is a castle in the sense that there are many large stone rooms and a surrounding moat. It is also like a maze for how I become lost. Everything looks the same wherever I go. I possess certain knowledge that I was not always alone, but I also know I am the last of my kind. Others were once with me fighting against the water as I am. It comes from the moat. It runs down the hallway or just outside, ready to pull one into its current. At any second it could suddenly flood a given room and take away its contents, including people. This is how each person disappeared in his turn. But it is not all random. Even as a group, we were significant in our like purpose. We were the last holdouts against being deposited in the valley below, dead or alive.

We held to certain principles. I've held mine all my life. I can recall how I held my ideas as I became a man. But a young man holds ideas in a much different way than an old man. It is largely due to how we hold our ideas that there was ever a war against us. Over time, mellowed by the siege and thanks to much experience, we were much more respectable, and the ideas too became a kind of heavenly fruit, but the die was cast, and we were hated. Bereft of ideas, the valley became cold and unrelenting in its quest to rid the fortress of us. Engineers used the power of the river and the structure of the moats, as well as the design of the castle, to devise a kind of trap to eliminate us. I alone remain having acquired the wisdom of how to beat the system, but as I run around, timing everything to keep from being swept away, I feel as if I'm some kind of pet in a prison, bounced around to the delight of the children peering in with their huge bulging eyes.

The Sanctuary

I'm in a nature sanctuary bordered by homes, something similar but much larger than a golf course, all covered with green, but the canopy lies on a great body of water that has been maintained and protected for many centuries. It undulates with the movements of creatures that are not poached nor studied. No one really knows what they look like, only that they have survived intact, or evolved over the millennia into this seething lagoon. I stand next to it in awe, watching as the canopy lifts up, bulges where huge creatures dart about, chasing after one another it seems, but unknown whether this is frolic or desperate flight at feeding time.

As I might discern it from my understanding of the jungle, I might assume that this is also all about survival of the fittest, and yet it feels like everything is healthy and thriving, including the entire canopy. I've never seen such health and vitality and abundance. This sanctuary has developed within our own world, and by comparison, ours is the one in a state of decadence and decay. The houses around the lagoon are surrounded in a mist not generated by the lagoon but by the airport, expressways and the city nearby.

I also have learned that gases from the lagoon have contributed as well to the general increased health of the region compared to other places, and now that we are in a state of ruin, scientists are demanding access to study it, to cut into the canopy and explore the depth of the water, to take samples and such, even at the risk of destroying a delicate balance and setting in motion the ultimate loss of this unique ecosystem, arguing that it will be worth it if we can learn from it how to save ourselves, which is unlikely since by dying we will lose what we do not even know with any certainty holds a cure. Part of me wants the canopy to rise and swallow us up to make the sanctuary cover the planet.

The Sports Car

My father is sitting in a small sports car that I hope will be mine someday. Sadly for me, he is not at all aware or sympathetic with the notion of passing things on to a son, at least not in the sense of taking care of anything. To him they are totally his, which of course they are, but there is also something cold and distant in that point of view, and I realize that he does nothing to have any kind of relationship with me. I do not feel like much of a son, nor do I feel very strongly that he is my father. In fact, I feel a kind of anger in general and in some ways hate both him and the car. As he sits there, I think, "Why doesn't he just drive over a cliff or something," and suddenly, there is such scenery. The car is sitting on a road having just come over a long bridge. My father puts on his sunglasses and sports cap, lights a cigarette and pulls the stick shift into reverse.

Then he slams his foot down on the gas, and the car wheels scream and screech as the vehicle races backwards towards the bridge. With just a few yards left, it leaves the road and rolls down the embankment over the cliff. I run to the edge and peer down, knowing he has gone to his doom, taking the car with him. I never wanted this, but in fact I had just wished for it. I call down to him, "Why did you do this to me?" but all I hear is an echo of those same words in his voice.

Driving Lesson

I am giving my daughter a driving lesson, but I am the only one doing the driving. It is a four lane street, two lanes going either way through the heart of the city, but everything is negative, similar to a photograph in infra-red black and white. The road is white with black lines and dashes marking the lanes, and the sky is very dark. I am going back and forth over the same span of road, but always towards the city. It is like being on the last clear area before the big buildings, something like going over a river, but either way I go, it is the same way by the look of the approaching skyscrapers.

It is out of this that I feel I must convey something important to my daughter. But what I honestly wish to tell her is only difficult to explain, not impossible to explain like the situation we're in, driving back and forth the same way. The problem is that usually I can at least translate a thought metaphorically; that is, I can approximate the meaning in some way. But here I am both lost and lost for words.

But this situation falls right into my fear, and to some extent right into reality. In one sense it is simple. "We are between two points, birth and death. We never actually blend in with the city per se. We only almost reach it, living on what we see of it even in the middle of it, which conflicts with our sense of it in totality from all we've heard and seen about it. At the same time, much of what we expect on the road of life is the opposite of what we get, and our whole life seems like a bridge to something, but we cannot figure out beginnings and endings." Yes, simple, but I can't explain it because she has the radio blasting and can't hear me.

The Bumblebee

I am a bumblebee and have grown thirsty after a long day of flying around during what has been a terrible drought. There are hardly any flowers, so there's very little nectar. I fly over a swimming pool and descend as I would to a watering hole or river, but there is no bank where I can land and approach, only an inflated rubber ring. I land on that and try to walk down to the water's edge, but my legs cannot find any grip, and I slide into the water. I hear screaming as a girl in the pool begins splashing water on me. She then puts a diving mask over me and pushes me to the bottom of the pool until I lose consciousness.

I wake paralyzed on top of a garbage can where the pool keeper is trying to revive me. It is his daughter in the pool, and she keeps crying for him to kill me. He tells her how important bees are and how their numbers are decreasing, but she wants me dead. I cannot move, but I also fear that she will get out of the pool and smash me if I show signs of life. I can now see through the eyes of the pool keeper and see that my legs are arched up as if I am reaching to heaven in the hope of being received.

I hear the pool keeper say to his daughter that my tiny legs are twitching. Indeed I see that they are through his eyes. Soon I see that he has picked up a dry reed of crabgrass and is trying to turn me over. He says he wants my wings to dry. I can see my legs are really moving now. Such signs of life, and I know from his daughter's words that I was underwater for quite some time. She cannot believe that I am not dead, but her father fears that perhaps the lack of oxygen has caused damage to me, and that I'll never gain all my strength to resume my normal life.

He keeps moving the garbage can to keep me in sunlight as long as possible, then finally takes his daughter away. Later he comes out, just before dark and sees that I'm still there, nearly fully restored. Finally he returns with a flashlight, and I am gone, but somehow I fear I've gotten lost in the dark. For me, darkness is a deep pool in which I feel I'll drown, but I have this light in my head that shows me the way home.

Bullies

I'm in my old hometown, the suburb I lived in until I was 15, torn from there I felt, when my family moved, turning the village into a kind of worshipful icon for me as all my friends and even the roads, houses and businesses became infused with my memories as a kind of pleasant and painful fizz drink that constantly tickled and itched my mind. I'm walking down my old street from my old house, past familiar dwellings, but already I'm feeling the familiar fear that lurks at the other end of the street where the Spectors lived, a mean family of bullies that wouldn't let me go down there without some kind of trouble, and yet it was my route to school, and I had to go that way every day.

I used to wait until the last minute, watch until I saw them leave for school. That way the street was empty when I passed their house. Sometimes I would still run into them as when one of them had forgotten something, and they would beat me up, so it was never a sure thing, and today I feel that same fear surge up again even though it has been many years.

As I near their house, I can see there are people in the front yard, and I can hear singing. Yes, they are singing, and the music is beautiful. As I near the house, I can see the old mean lady, the mother, is now in a wheelchair. The boy my age, who always betrayed me when I did try to be his friend from time to time over the years growing up there, is beside her; and next to him is his ruthless brother, the leader of the gang. He is taking the lead solo, and what a range he has!

Hearing their chorus reminds me of what a great music program we had in this town. I was always singled out for solos, told that I would succeed, that my voice was special, but we moved to a place where music was not important. Now I see what I might have been and what I might have done if we hadn't left, and I feel bullied even now, that this song is one of deliberate, in-your-face intimidation, a perfect selection for a hated visitor.

I walk by shielding my face, hoping they will not recognize me, and based on the past, I do not for a minute think they have changed because the music is heavenly. I know they are up to something and wish I had a brick to throw and disrupt the song.

The View

I am the caretaker of an historical landmark, a house where one of our greatest founding fathers often slept, and not only is it my job to keep everything in the house exactly as was from the time the great man was there, but it is equally important that the view from the window be maintained in strict accordance with the paintings that have always been in the house, even when our great founder was there, and some say that he even painted them.

Looking at the paintings and looking through the window is one of the delights of visiting the house. In any season one can match the outside view to a painting because so many were done. There are several from each season in different kinds of weather at different times of day.

When asked by a visitor, I am hard-pressed to say that I have ever seen a view that I could not match to a painting, and I joke that of course at times the clouds do seem a little off. There's even one of an eclipse, and one for every phase of the moon, and even among the visitors no one has ever said after a tour that there was no match.

The grounds outside the window though are the hardest part of my job. The view stretches to the horizon, so all the shrubs and trees have to be the correct position and right perspective, sized in the same way they appear in the paintings. We have a tree and shrub nursery to help with this. If the wind were ever to blow over a tree, then we can replace it quickly with one that looks the same. It is a great job, and I am the 30th caretaker in a line stretching back hundreds of years, and there has never been a problem, until now.

Yesterday someone pointed out an anomaly on the horizon, something that is not correct in the pictures. Upon investigating, it turns out that a new skyscraper, the tallest building in the world, is going up more than 100 miles away. I have called to confirm, and it appears the building is far from complete, and by the time it is finished, it will stick up on the horizon like an obelisk from the future, piercing and denigrating our pristine nook set apart from time.

I called, and the owner of the building under construction laughed when I suggested he scale it back so that we can't see it. He knows of us and has been here, but as a result of my call, he is promising to do paintings from the town and maintain a look all the way out to the horizon where he hopes we will still be in the picture for 1000 years if he doesn't buy us up first and tear us down.

I hung up the phone. Later, I consider in a panic that perhaps we can block the view of the finished building with a tree, and add the new tree to all the paintings.

The Proof

I am given an ultimatum by the Lords of the Council that may end up killing me, which is to fulfill my promise to write equations that prove their model for the universe, which I have long known to be false. I even have the equations to prove it, but the reason it may kill me is that it is heresy to question their authority let alone bring down their entire architecture of thought in a single proof. So either way, it is my head.

I cannot fake an equation proving their model is true because they would easily detect a flaw, and I cannot present a proof that their model is false because they would detect its veracity and arrest me, then destroy the proof. Then it occurs to me that they already know their model is false. I mean, how could they not know it? Hard as it would be to publish the truth, as much as it would disrupt society, still, these are the leaders of our culture in intellectual pursuit. They must know it, and yet they must protect it. So perhaps they have somehow gathered that I know their model is false and wish to expose and do away with me.

Actually, this test is a perfectly contrived trap, and I can't see how I can save myself other than to make some kind of move to join the Council. The problem there is that the line of succession requires a death before a new Lord can be initiated. These men have their seats for life, and there are numerous elders ahead of me waiting their turn.

In order to gain a seat on the Council, I would need to pretty much decimate the entire chamber, which would certainly leave me exposed, but on the other hand, I might flow into the chamber in the line of succession without my crime being discovered.

I do believe it is time for a schism, and that I must determine who is with me, then start a new Council with a new model. I hate to be the cause of a war, but my model is simple and will be seen as true by the common man. My only fear is whether I will ever get out of the castle alive because looking out the window, I already see all the Lords and elders coming in a procession. Either this is some kind of new procession, or I am toast.

Neighbors

I am caught in a terrible and chaotic rush-hour traffic jam on the highway far from home when I happen to catch sight of one of my neighbors in his car several lanes over trapped in the same mess. I start waving, but I am in a small car with shaded windows, and he's not even looking my way. I doubt he would ever see me through the window anyway, and to have more room to wave, I roll it down, and a waft of awful heat invades the interior. I am quickly uncomfortable and roll the window back up.

I lower the thermostat to cool off the car, but it stays hot. I noticed my neighbor seems happy and comfortable enough in his car, which is a convertible. I also see he's moved up a few car lengths because I can only see the back of his head now.

I try to move over to the next lane, but we are stopped dead and nobody will let me in. As traffic does move from time to time, all of my focus is on moving over and following my neighbor, to get close enough to get his attention, but nothing works. When I do manage to change to another lane, it goes more slowly than the one I was in.

Meanwhile, my neighbor keeps moving ahead by another car length or two. He is still close, but too far to expect to get his attention anymore. I also cannot leave the car and walk to him as we move too often for that, even if only a few feet at a time. Also, I wouldn't go that far because I actually don't like my neighbor very much, nor do I get along with him very well. It's just that out here in this sea of automobiles on the hot pavement, it is quite a coincidence and might be a good thing for both of us to have a good laugh under the circumstances, which might ease tensions a little once we're both back in the neighborhood. I'm only trying to be neighborly here, but I'm also cutting people off, moving in and out of lanes, somehow always the wrong one.

Meanwhile my neighbor stays in his lane, always advancing, though no more than 10 or 12 cars ahead even after an hour of this. The only lane I don't want to be in is his because then I would always be behind him and never catch up.

Finally traffic begins to move faster. I see it's an accident that caused the jam. I drive faster but can't see my neighbor anywhere. When I get home, he ignores me and vise versa as usual. I like him even less than before. When I get in the house, the phone is ringing. It's my wife. She's had an accident. She was in the car I passed. She said she saw me and waved like crazy to get my attention, but I drove past her like a mindless idiot.

Solitude

I find myself on the ground in the middle of the woods and pick myself up to see several liquor bottles lying there with grass growing up between them. A little further away sitting against a tree is an old rusted shotgun. I pick it up, and it falls apart in my hands. I feel hazy and hungry, so I go down the hill to the village, which seems busier than usual, even strange to my eyes. I go to the coffee shop and get some coffee where the clerk calls me "old-timer" and comments that the coins I give him are very old indeed.

After that I head home and go through a busted gate and tall grass into the house. There are two rather large and unfriendly women where I expected to find my beautiful wife and cute little daughter. After some heated words from the older and fatter of the two, about fixing the gate and mowing the lawn, I realize that this is my wife, and I stare carefully at the other fat woman with pimples all over her face, and I'm shocked to realize that behind all that ugliness is my daughter, some 20 or 30 years older than when I last saw her.

I head to a mirror and take a look at myself and realize I must have just done a Rip van Winkle because I'm all old and gray. But then why are they not surprised and excited to see me? My wife then goes into a rant about how much I drink, and how she's sick of it. My daughter cries that I've done nothing but ruin her life, that she could have been talented and played the piano, but instead she stays home eating fudge because she's ashamed to go out and listen to her former friends tease her about her drunken father.

I listen to the two of them haranguing and insulting me for several hours, grabbing a few bites to eat while they take turns berating me, and slowly, little by little, some of it starts to come back to me. I begin to feel that maybe in fact I might remember that this is my home, and I am in the present. But no, it can't be! I listen to this enough and can't take any more abuse.

I lock myself in a back bedroom and find what's left of an old coin collection hidden under the bed. I hear pounding on the door as I pocket some of the coins and push the rest of the collection back where it was. My wife and daughter are yelling and screaming at me to open the door, but I climb out the window and head to the liquor store where I buy several bottles of booze and pocket the few coins I have left, then amble up the hill to the deep forest for some peace and quiet.

The Hoarder

I am an old man living in squalor but have a few specific people in mind to blame for my circumstances, and as much as their actions have kept me down and out, they have risen to such heights that to do them harm in retaliation would be an event of historical proportions, which just happens to coincide with a desire I have to do something important and historical that will change the world even if it means that I will be remembered as a villain. So I start to make a plan of how I will do the deed, but I keep it all in my head and tell no one, knowing that if even the slightest whiff of it gets out, it would be thwarted. I also know that once it's done, the authorities will burst into my house and begin a search through everything I have, so as part of my ingenious and complex plan, I meticulously delete all my e-mail messages from my accounts and wipe my computer's hard drive clean.

I also go through all my file cabinets and burn what amounts to more than half a century of documents I've saved through the years, from high school notes passed in class to all current paperwork of any kind. This is really a massive collection and it takes days to haul it out and burn it, but I don't want them to know anything about me regarding past associates or interests that would cause them to contact people I haven't seen in ages and ask them to speculate about me. Then I remove the huge piles of newspapers and magazines I've saved over the years, each containing an article that riled me up, fueling my rage bit by bit over the years.

I also clean out every room including the garage of all the things I obviously won't need once I am hauled away to prison, and this is where the job is really time-consuming and difficult. I have always been a pack rat, and there is just so much stuff that I've accumulated over the years, so much that it has been hard to move around the house, which has been very depressing.

Removing the squalor takes weeks to complete, but in the end, I only keep a "few mean sticks of furniture" as they say, necessities for daily living, and nothing else. I also spiff up the exterior, paint the house, and mow the lawn as I don't want them driving up and conjecturing that I'm some kind of slob.

When it's all done I can't believe it. I walk around the house now and can hear an echo. I threw out the carpet so my footsteps are loud, even in my stocking feet. It's like a whole new house, a whole new world, a whole new life, and I feel a happiness I haven't felt in years. Then I recall there was something I wanted to do that seems very complicated, but I can't remember what it was. What I've just managed to accomplish was complicated enough for an old man like myself, it seems to me, and I wind up on a rocking chair on my porch enjoying the sunset, not just of the day, but of my whole life.

Bookmark

I am a butterfly, and somehow I know that I am very rare, maybe even one of the last if not the last of my kind. I would say I knew this instinctively, but actually I've been flying around for such a long time that I should have found another of my species by now, but there's been nothing, not even the faintest trace of a scent of pheromone in the air, so I've come to realize that I am rare and unique by experience as well.

I've also noticed that depending on where I fly, there is quite a bit of interest generated in the scientific community. I once landed on a window, and I noticed how the man in the office quickly picked up the phone and made a call. Almost immediately, there were trucks and cars below all pulling up with people getting out and looking up, and it took me quite a while to lose them because even in the park where there are trees, it's easy enough to spot which one I am in, so I actually had to go across the river out of this city before I found an area without roads and was finally able to land on a branch and rest, so tired was I after that chase.

And that was only one of many. For you see they won't give up. They have spotters all over the perimeter of the woods waiting for me to come out. Two or three times I've been seen and another chase ensued, even on foot in the woods, below me, somehow able to keep up with me until I managed to get above the canopy and catch a fortunate gust of wind that took me all the way up a hill.

I am reaching the point where I have to make a decision what to do, where to go, and it seems my best bet for survival is to seek sanctuary with a particular type of group of people other than the scientists. The group I'm considering is known first and foremost for its innocence. For some reason this type of person is by nature very loving regarding butterflies as they even have books about them enjoyed by this class of people known as "children."

I've always wanted to be in a book, so I decide to make my way into the midst of this innocent group the next time I am pursued. I don't have to wait long as I'm spotted and driven out of the woods, back across the river and into the city by a smokescreen from a fire made deliberately for this purpose. Lucky for me, I spy a large gathering of children in a schoolyard. I land among them and see the joy on their faces just before they capture and slam a book shut on me so that I'm smashed somewhere in the middle between its pages.

The Firing

I am a waiter in a restaurant arriving at work on a great wave of a sense that somehow the mind not only connects, but is on top of everything, in control, and that all things almost seem to flow out of it. As I walk inside, a customer I know obviously doesn't recognize me but detects my cogent, confident aura and moves to leave a seat for me, hoping I'll sit down and grace the company with my presence. I must decline. Further down, there sits a bubbling conversationalist as usual, a young beauty who is a regular, talking about a famous UFO code-named "Pearson," and she is just at the point where she is trying to remember where it is supposedly from, and just as I walk by, I throw in "Jupiter," which is the correct answer. The way she is surprised and thanks me delightedly, I know I'll be closer with her later. Out in back, I reach the locker/apartment area where we live and store our things.

Just before I go in my apartment, I'm met by one of the other waiters who says humorously, "Is there any way that we could finally and ultimately intertwine our lives and effectively become one?"

"I don't know," I answer, "but wherever it goes, let me start by giving you back all your jewelry," and I take what are his things out of my pocket, some necklaces and rings, which he gave me in a hurry and asked me to hold for him the night before. The joke is not lost on him, and we share a good laugh at the repartee. The necklaces are somewhat tangled though, with my own, and he says it's okay, that he'll wear one of mine, but I say, no, I'll untangle them.

His is like a small silver cinder block with four holes that I recall stringing up myself though I forgot how I did it. In the worst case, I could break the string and redo it from the roll of string in my locker. He keeps saying he'll wear my stuff, and I say, no, to give me a minute.

At that moment when I am concentrating completely on untangling the necklaces, the garbage men arrive to empty the bins and collect the bags gathered about. I seem to keep getting in their way and move around for them each time they return, having to reset and start over with the untangling process. Finally I give up and break the string and start to try to restring the necklace, but I'm having trouble. He takes my necklace and says he doesn't want to be late. I'll only be a few minutes, I tell him, and that's when I see the pink slip on my locker informing me that my tardiness no longer will be tolerated. I've been evicted, and the garbage men have just taken away all my belongings.

Typecast

I am an actor who always plays the villain, advocate of some dying method or old school way of thinking, pressing and harassing the hero until finally defeated in the end. I was the teacher that would rap the knuckles of the child with a ruler. I played the abusive priest, the hospital administrator wanting to pull the plug on the patient, the rancher who hired a gunslinger to drive homesteaders off their ranches. In any event, it was just by looking at me that made the audience turn against me. They detected my point of view from the look in my eye. I was the vile one, and I was successful in these roles.

But over time, always associated with negative things and always getting my parts due to my demeanor, I honestly began to question my existence. What was I that I could stir up such hatred and negative emotions? What was it that I believed that would naturally be considered to be a wrong way of thinking? I found myself in many of the roles being sympathetic to the character I played. It was the method where I got the most out of myself. I played them to the hilt. When defeated, I told myself that movies must end that way, and that in life people like me are more often victorious. You don't have to be well-liked to get ahead. Take how I snaked my way into the studios, convincing people, backstabbing associates with more experience, doing whatever I had to do to get ahead until I got the parts I wanted. Sure, I played hardball, but still, in the twilight of my career, people see me and congratulate me as if I were one of their heroes. They don't see me as the person in those roles, but only as an actor. But I feel if they honestly knew my heart, then they would in fact hate me.

And so I hate them though I smile and sign autographs at premier events, even though I tell the truth about myself constantly on screen, turning down roles of the softhearted guy who usually wins because I never could put my heart into such a part, never could believe it was me no matter how hard I try. Not that I wouldn't get the girl. I got plenty of those. But in the films, when I lose her to the good guy who rides off victoriously, I am solaced by the fact that it doesn't always work out that way in life, that bad guys like me do win. I am a villain at heart but beloved by all despite effortlessly and expertly making everyone cringe and despise me.

The Alligator

I am seeing a side of people that I have never seen before, and at first glance, it strikes me that there has been a kind of evolutionary shift in the form of the body, but then I realize that I am not viewing people in the physical world, but on the psychic, or spiritual plane. Here the forms are set up differently. I don't know whether this spiritual/psychic form is the result of evolution or experience. The reason I say that is it appears it is more pronounced in some than others.

A good example of this is my friend, a kind of twin in many respects. I have managed somehow to offend him. I couldn't see that in the physical world except in the changed tone of his voice. The other cues such as a facial expression or gestures were not visible because we were on the phone when the altercation happened. It really didn't matter whether I could see him physically or not, to recognize the spiritual or psychic form after that.

In this form of mind, between the psychic and physical world, the spirit has a shape similar to a massive alligator where the eyes are set so that they can peer out on the surface where information is mutually visible, clear and shared in the physical world. There is also the murkiness of the silent unknown, particular to every soul, just beneath that in the psychic world. We all know how to descend into those dark depths and leave others wondering what became of us. We can also work on the surface and snap at any time.

The analogy to the alligator is also accurate in terms of the nature of the beast itself. Physically my head and body are best suited to land and air, to moderate temperatures and altitudes. But in spirit, I do well and am quite fit for lurking just at the surface. I can disappear in an instant into depths unknown, and I can reappear to bite your head off any time I wish.

Old Influences

I have gone to visit the old homestead, my boyhood home, and I find that it is actually vacant and for sale. I often come back here looking for answers as to why my siblings seem better adjusted than me. They seem fine and moved away while I stuck around in the area.

For many reasons, childhood was particularly difficult for me, but mainly I've never seemed to have gotten beyond or forgotten all the punishments bestowed on me by parents hell bent on correction.

As I stand in front of the house, it doesn't seem like anyone is around, so I walk to the backyard and sit down for a while to wait in case someone saw me and comes back to check on me. I don't know why, but being here not only brings back lots of memories, but I am also experiencing a certain familiar sense that I'm in trouble somehow and shouldn't be out here, as if my late mother is still at the helm, the driving force of my life, focussed on enforcing her many rules.

I usually shake off this feeling fairly easily, but today it seems stronger and is hanging on for some reason. It makes it easy to recall how often I would be in trouble back in the same place for little things, and over the years how trained I became, as a result, to keep in mind all of her rules.

After maybe fifteen minutes of sitting there, the coast seems clear enough, and I check the windows, discovering the bathroom window is actually open enough for me to push myself up and squeeze my way through into the house. It is completely empty except for a cardboard box here and there. There are some extra tiles where someone has apparently finished tiling the floor.

The house seems bigger than I remember, which is strange because I've always thought on previous occasions driving by that it seemed smaller. But this is the first time I've been inside in many years, so perhaps that has something to do with it. Also the furnishings are gone, and its being empty is a factor.

As I look around, I remember my father had a concealed entrance into a secret attic, which he sealed when we moved. I find the area and test what I remember and find the seal is intact. I remove it and enter an area that is still pristine. Nobody has been here since we moved out, and I was never allowed up here as a boy, so this is all totally new to me.

Again, that familiar feeling of doing something wrong comes back to me. Looking around, I find my old box of baseball cards and other toys that I thought had disappeared. Obviously, my parents just plain took them away and hid them from me up here. I look around for what else there is, and I find a strange device that looks like a pop-corn machine. There is a set of viewer lenses, a place for someone to press his head and look through, similar to a swimming mask, and I realize that this is a subliminal generator, something that is used to view a film for example, and insert subliminal message placements into specific spots in a film, wherever the editor wishes. Basically, this abomination of a device creates a link to the subconscious mind with subliminal messages embedded at intervals to be transmitted back in a continuous loop.

There's a box next to the machine containing old cartridges the machine uses. I look at the labels and discover that these are actually the spiritual mindsets of my siblings. I had wished to select my own mind-print and watch it in slow-motion, but I cannot find one.

But I understand the implications here, and to my great sadness realize my mother inserted her rules and warnings liberally and to excess, so much that while examining the machine, I look up now and then in extreme fear for the terrible wrong I'm doing to be here, discovering what my parents did to control us. It's then I notice that the machine was left on all these years, and the reason I could not find the cartridge aimed for my mind is that it was left in the machine, continuously sending subliminal messages to me all these many years as I never left its range. This corresponds to my parents' rule that I stay close to home or suffer the consequences.

Smooth World

I have been transferred to a place called, "Smooth World," where life is very different. There are already millions of people here, and millions more arriving every day. There is a complete eviction of the entire earth going on, and within a few months, everyone will be on "Smooth World."

The thing about this place that I first noticed was how fitting the name is. Everything really is smooth. It's all about the technology. Earth was basically organic to the core and prone to wetness and overgrowth like ivy growing out of control all over the place. Something was always getting into the wires, and the environments and weather variations made producing a viable infrastructure impossible.

But here, teams started arriving many years ago and began making the infrastructure, putting everything in place for the day of crossover when we would leave that organic ball of decay for our new home in a land of wonder. That's what we were told anyway, and now that I'm here, I can see what they were talking about.

Everyone is having a great time as far as I can see. I am in the new arrival area, and people are sliding around on their stocking feet, enjoying how smooth everything is. I also hear voices declaring the magnificence and perfection of the place. I take off my shoes to join in the fun, and when I drop one to the floor, the noise is different. It's as if a sound has been added where no sound was.

I drop the other shoe, and the same thing happens. It is similar to turning a smart phone off and on. The device makes no sound of its own really, but plays an electronic placebo click that differentiates whatever you're doing. That's what's happening everywhere here on Smooth World. I open the door, and there's a nice sound of a door opening played for me, with no squeaks ever! That is so wonderful!

After a while of sliding around and tapping things to hear the various electronic supplements for real sounds, I'm starting to get a bit tired of it all as my turn at processing finally approaches. I turn to the next guy to say I'm getting tired, but what comes out of my mouth is, "Isn't this place great? What a wonderful world!"

That isn't what I'd wanted to say. His answer is in kind, praising the place, but his lips are moving in a different way, and there is consternation on his face.

As we go through processing, we continue to hear the voices of praise, but the faces have all turned unhappy, and as we enter the next area, what looks like a wailing and gnashing of teeth has a musical background, and a delightful cacophony of an overjoyed throng.

In the Elements

I am Pinocchio, and I open my eyes to see that I am on a train with a group of boys familiar to me for having seen them at the carnival or "Land of the Boobies" as it's called in the book. I'm very cold, and I feel my nose, which is also very cold, and while it's obvious given its length that I've told a few lies, I am able to warm it with my hands and don't want it getting any longer for fear it will freeze, so I promise myself to stick to the facts from here on out. I ask one of the boys what happened, and he tells me that we were all at the carnival when a huge dogfish came out of the sea and swallowed every last one of us.

He says that I was knocked out, and the other boys dragged me on the train so I wouldn't miss the ride. I ask where we are going, and he answers, "To the dogs."

As soon as he says that, there's a sudden increase in the noise and tension on the train. The boys who were relatively peaceful and quiet begin acting up a bit more, breaking things and such. "But I thought we were supposed to turn to donkeys, not go to the dogs," I tell him.

"Well that's all changed now," he replies. "Maybe it's the salt water bath we took when the fish swallowed us."

Then I feel I can ask him why it's so cold. I'm feeling really frozen to death. "I thought this was supposed to be a whole whale. Aren't whales warm-blooded?"

"I told you it's a dogfish," he answers. "Didn't you read the story? It's cold blooded. Very cold indeed. About the coldest beast there is, and we're heading into the belly of a dogfish, going to the dogs." Again, the boys turn it up a notch when he says we're going to the dogs, breaking more things, being more violent.

"Can it be that big that we could actually be on the train?" I turn to him and ask.

"Hey, the book said it was two miles long, but I think that's an understatement."

I feel the train start to slow down and look out the window. The front cars are turning on a trestle that overlooks a snowy plain that almost seems to be glowing in the darkness. It is literally covered with many hundreds, maybe thousands of animals, which I realize are ravenous wolves.

The cars turn out to be hopper cars where the bottoms open and empty their contents. One after another, each car moves up, opens at the bottom and shakes out all the boys to the waiting, hungry wolves below. "This isn't happening! This isn't happening!" I keep saying, watching my nose grow longer and longer. My car is next, and I keep waiting for either supernatural or parental intervention to save me, but there's no help for me.

Family Quarrel

I catch my daughter with a boy I told her not to see, and we get into an argument. I lose my temper and begin to spout off rules that must be followed, sputtering and shouting, which causes her to cry. She threatens to continue seeing the boy, saying that I cannot tell her what to do, which infuriates me into that area where there are spasmodic/reflex reactions that have no forethought. I lash out at her and swing my hand to hit her, and my hand goes through her chest into her body.

What follows horrifies me as I feel my hand being torn apart as if it has been caught in the gears of a machine. I yank it out as quickly as possible, but I see immediately that four of my fingers have been ripped off, which explains the terrible pain. We are both treated at the hospital, and when our bandages come off around the same time, my hand looks like a thumb on a stump, and my daughter barely has a scar on her chest.

Our relationship seems alright after that and she maintains the kind of obedience and respect I've always asked for. She does her chores and comes and goes always with an explanation of her plans, and she is always on time, but somehow her personality has changed. She is not quite as interesting, and she seems sad all the time, or to describe it better, her mood is always gray or monotone.

This affects her friendships and social life, and where she used to be very popular, now she sits at home all the time, watching television and eating snacks. She grows obese and lethargic, and I wind up taking care of her as she can't hold down a job. As I grow old, I feel I am still having to help her more than she helps me. In some way I want to slap her back to what she was, but it is too late for that, and an angry outburst which I regret has always seemed to be where her personality took a turn for the worse.

Alone and unmarried, she finally gets sick one day and dies. I am overwhelmed with grief already, but to make matters worse, I am brought in to watch the autopsy and witness the medical examiner extracting four fingers that he says were gumming up her works all these years, wrapped around her throat in such a way as to severely limit her prospects for having any future.

The Slave

I know I do not want to be a slave, but though a way seems clear and easy where I could make my escape, I choose to sit and do the work assigned to me each day by my guard who spends much of his time barking at me and cracking his whip over me. Many of these whip cracks have landed on me over the years as I have the scars to prove it, but generally at this point of my life, the whip cracking is for show as he tries to impress his overseer, and only on occasion does one of these actually strike me, in which case I may wince a little but show no other sign of distress and get on with my work.

The path to freedom is more like a beam of sunlight than a road out of here, but I know I could easily and at any time deliquesce and ride up into the light despite the guard watching over me and the chains on my ankles and wrists, keeping me tied to the table where I work. I do not know how I know that "deliquesce" is the right word. I do know that this word offers as good an approximation as any word for what would actually transpire should I try to escape. The word "melt" is inadequate, and it isn't about the spirit leaving the body.

I think one has to have been a slave over an entire lifetime and tattooed with whip scars to really understand the difference. The light path only appears after a certain term of dues paying in that regard, and I can even see it at night coming through the window like moonlight on a moonless evening. This light comes right through the walls, and I bask my feet in it, and it gives me great strength and comfort.

Still I feel I must get back to that table in the morning. I am driven to it. I cannot help myself. The light keeps calling me, but I have so much to do at the table. It is where I really lose myself completely, and it's only in light of the light that I see my slavery. It shines on my work and reveals a complete lack of understanding, which causes the guard to crack his whip, and I get working again. Only when I turn my back on the light does the guard stop with the whip and my work come out of the shadows.

Desert Command

I am captain of a desert ship and have managed to get lost somewhere on this vast deck of sand. The ship spans hundreds of miles and basically carries the entire desert, but it is like any other ship, a machine that is managed by our crew, well trained in procedures of the corps. I myself went through many years of training at the academy and rose through the ranks on similar vessels, and I was very proud to take command of my own ship, the vastness of which has everything to do with my many years of proud service.

Lost out here, it has been a long time since I have seen another soul. I've gone over dune after dune and have seen nobody. I haven't even encountered a footprint. The wind seems to take care of that. Occasionally, I believe I see an oasis, but mirages are quite common as well. The conning tower and gun turrets are each disguised as an oasis as well, so I do take such sightings seriously. But following them, everything I've seen has turned out to be your garden-variety mirage.

I have plenty of provisions to last me quite a while, which is a fact I credit to my years of training and service. I would not be out here at all if I didn't know exactly what I am doing. Even "being lost" is a part of desert command. It is a daily exercise. If I did not find a way to be lost at the beginning of a shift, I would not be fit for command. It is only in navigating in this way that the entire desert ship has focus and moves according to the master plan, which is a secret handed down through command headquarters on a need-to-know basis.

As captain, this information is for my eyes only as I begin my day. But my moments through the desert on deck are all recorded. When I find my way back, the log entries are adjusted to include the new matrix of my escape and recovery, whereupon there is a new and total readjustment of the ship's design and heading such that whether there be ravages of wind where sandstorms rage and seemingly readjust an entire landscape, our bearings will still be clear, the mission intact.

Now I come upon my bones from yesterday's trek, so I know I'm on the right track. Amazing how quickly the sun and sand have bleached them. I'll go from here where the fingers on my skeleton's hand are pointing the way to tomorrow. I love this desert commission, and I wouldn't trade it for all the green in the world.

Product Talk

I am walking downstairs in low light, and I'm startled by strange noises. There seem to be voices talking to me. I scamper back up to the hallway and flip on the light, and I see only a few odds and ends like laundry detergent and folded clothes. As I go back down, slowly this time, I hear the voices again, first from a bottle of laundry detergent telling me how great the product is and how clean my clothes will be, and next from a bag of decaffeinated coffee reminding me it is nearing coffee time, asking why don't I brew a cup using this bag. The product has a blue ribbon on it, and in the blue circle, there is a video of a face talking to me.

I move back a few steps, and the voices stop again, and I surmise they are proximity activated, but I wonder why I didn't notice them before. I go to the kitchen and open the cabinet and am met with a confused chorus of voices, each telling me to use whatever product they represent. Some have music. Most have their own animation of a spokesperson talking up the product. I find this form of advertising obtrusive and alarming.

Just then, my wife comes in the door carrying bags of products from the grocery store, all yelling for attention. She is completely out of energy and heads to the bedroom, telling me to get the rest out of the car and to put them all away. I go to the car, and my approach activates a chorus of voices in the bags that I carry into the house. Some of the jingles they sing are familiar, and I find myself hungry for a cookie. Once in the kitchen again, I rip open the packaging, and a voice says, "Ouch!" followed by "Just kidding."

Later, my wife and I go to the one room in the house free of all products to watch television, where we hear that soon the degree of product voicing will be expanded to include towels, sheets and clothing, and that everyone we pass will basically have their clothes tell us what brands they are wearing and how comfortable they fit. It appears that only one state in the country is fighting this, and so far it has been successful in keeping the products off its shelves. My wife says she wants to move there.

Then we hear on the news that the governor of that state was just killed in an automobile crash. His wife, who survived, said they had just gotten the car back from repairs, and halfway home the dashboard lit up and started calling him names. Then the steering wheel literally refused to move, and they went off the road. At this point the TV shuts off and declares that it's time for us to go to bed.

A Perfect Life

I am standing at the top of a flight of stairs, and I have this feeling that I'm about to fall if everything in my life is perfect. At first, it seems easy enough to project that I'll be able to walk away at first consideration, but I can't seem to find anything wrong, not the tiniest flaw in my life. I remember working very hard over these last 10 years or so to make amends and fix things up; in short, do anything and everything it takes to ensure everything is right, everyone is happy, and that there are no loose ends.

Realizing this, I can feel myself start to teeter over the edge of the top stair. But I pull myself back with all my strength and tell myself that this was just a first pass, a cursory glance, that no life is perfect, and something must turn up. But alas, using every tool available to any person or agency, all of my paperwork comes up clean. Every score is among the highest in every category, and there are testimonials as well from bona fide bulletproof references.

Again, I can feel myself leaning toward a full somersault to my doom at the bottom of the stairs. But then I tell myself, there must be some mistake, that I must be hiding something. Just then, in the back of my mind, almost as if in a hidden closet somewhere, under a carpet and under the floorboards, I have a sense that something does exist, but I do not know what it is, and I've obviously buried it so well that I can't be sure if I'm not at this moment making it up to keep from falling.

Then I almost tip over and catch myself on the handrail, and it all comes back to me. Yes, it's huge, not just one thing but a gigantic sack of lies that completely refutes the whole perfect legacy thing, changing my life from top to bottom. Grateful to go on living, I say thank God I am reprieved and breathe a sigh of relief that my many terrible transgressions have disgraced and saved me.

Map of Flowers

I have enhanced vision and am able to see into a flower to the beauty and complexity of its very genome, and I am overwhelmed by the sheer magnificence that goes far beyond anything that has been seen in the human counterpart. This witnessing puts me in mind of the biblical verse in Matthew Chapter 6 that says, "Even Solomon in all his splendor was not arrayed as one of these," in reference to the lilies of the field. This underlying recognition of the inner makeup of the simple flower is exactly what I'm bowled over by, and I decide it would be a wondrous achievement to document and depict it in a picture so that all can appreciate it.

So I set out to painstakingly map the flower's genome, painting it just as it is, and I have to start very small because of how elaborate and gigantic it actually is. The project takes a long time, but many years later when I am nearing completion of the enlarged depiction of this infinitesimally small thing, I happen to be standing back from it and catch sight of the huge canvas, and I'm taken aback by the fact that I see nothing that could be comprehended or reconciled to be a flower. It would be like making a photographic slide of every cell in the human body, stacking them on top of one another, and shining a light through the stack and expecting some kind of revelation to appear on the dark screen.

I sit and wonder what I did wrong and cannot understand how the map of the flower's genome does not convey the beauty and grandeur that I clearly see in comprehending it with my enhanced vision. Why does it not come through, I wonder. I consider that perhaps it would be like taking a face off a skull and turning it around to look at it from the side where all the blood vessels and muscles are exposed, things that obviously add to the beauty in some way but are not themselves beautiful to behold, even if one finds beauty in the conceptualization of the magnificent complexity of the human body that takes it far beyond the possibility that it could ever have happened by accident.

This is exactly what I had wanted to show with the flower. I spent many years in what has obviously been a huge failure when all I wanted was to convey what was for me a transforming and transcendent religious experience. I wanted to create something that would allow that to happen for others, to grasp that inner profundity. Extracting and displaying it, I thought, would be all I would need to do. But alas, it turned out to be like a child picking this simple beautiful flower, not knowing it would soon wither and die; the beautiful little flower that touches us with its frailty without bragging about, or being blinded by, its majestic heart.

The Pit

I am a little boy listening to my father give someone directions. They have stopped in front of our house and are lost. My father quickly loses me as he explains the route they should follow. Beyond a couple of streets away, I don't know my way around. One thing he says comes as a surprise to me. He mentions a thing called, "The Pit." He says they should watch out for it. I'm not sure if he means they should be careful or use it as a landmark, but I've not heard of the pit before.

As with some things that happen in youth, the first time one hears a term just activates the ears to recognize it going forward. That night at dinner my mother says something about the pit, and my father mentions that he gave directions to some people who were lost, to which my mother says she hopes he did not forget to mention the pit. I turn and ask my father what the pit is, and his answer is, "Nothing you need to concern yourself with now."

I feel dissatisfied with this explanation, but I know enough not to pursue it further based on his tone. But I am still very curious, and that night as I look out my bedroom window, kneeling on my bed, I wonder where the pit is out there. Is it straight ahead? Do roads just go into it without warning? Will I accidentally go into it if I disobey and ride my bike beyond the designated limit?

Over the next several years, I hear references to the pit more often. My ears go up whenever I hear the use of the term. I manage to catalog them into a kind of summary that indicates it is very close by, and that it is vast, yet somewhat easy to miss. One can ride along its edge and miss the fact it is there simply because a few rows of trees completely block it. Many people have been lost in it. In fact, it seems that it is far more unusual to meet one's demise without the pit being involved than for the pit to not be in any given story of doom.

I finally ask my father if he will take me to the pit and show it to me, to which he responds that one day he will, but before he gets a chance, one night he doesn't come home, and my mother cries that the pit got him.

Too Close to the Son

I am Icarus, but not like you think. The truth is that I never actually made the trip with my father Daedalus. He made his wings and mine, and he flew off the prison island and eventually made it to safety, but I was too frightened to even take off, and so I stayed and served my term on the island prison, where I stocked food and ate my fill, growing rather plump in the process. By the time I was released, and able to sail on a ship to our home, my father was even older. I mean it wasn't even like it was him. Though he was the most important man of the society, with a house on a beautiful ledge jutting out over the sea, he was sick and frail, much of his condition attributed to me and exacerbated by the ordeal of having a coward for a son.

Upon my return, there was great astonishment and jubilation. Everyone except my father was amazed that I was alive, and they wondered how it was that I was so healthy. My father diverted their attention from this and pretended to be happy. He even said, "Now I can die in peace!" But the truth was that he wished I'd never come home. "Why didn't you just stay a myth?" he cried, and I didn't know what he was talking about.

Then, as he explained it to me, it all started to make sense. Everyone took me for being lost at sea for having flown too close to the sun, a tale he wove on arrival to save face and create some kind of acceptable fate for me. That fictional fate was just credited to an overabundance of youth. People could understand that. They even had sympathy for me. They saw it in their own children. Now add to that notoriety the fact that they believed I had somehow survived a tragic fall from the sky into the ocean. I would have had to have swum a long way, or maybe I was picked up by a passing ship. What was it, they wanted to know. What were my adventures, they asked, expecting to hear a tale like the one of brave Ulysses and the years it took him to return to Ithaca.

I realized I had to tell them something, but I knew they understood I was exhausted after my ordeal, and I promised that I would tell them everything after a few days of rest. They agreed and word went around that I would soon address the people. Meanwhile I ran to my father who was at his house standing on the ledge contemplating the sunset. I asked him what I should do. He said the best thing to do was to run, to take his old set of wings he used to escape, put them on and get as far away as I could as fast as I could. He even recommended that I fly too close to the sun and fulfill my destiny.

These harsh words hit a little too close to the "son," as it were, meaning me. I had just put on the wings and could feel the feathers ruffle. In anger I pushed my father over the ledge where he fell into the sea. As the people came, I tried to fly but was too heavy. They arrested me and put me in prison. Well, I guess I always was and will always be a jailbird.

Lunar Program

I hear that a new program has begun to recruit people to go to the moon, which is something I'd always dreamed of doing since I was a boy. I remember looking out the window to the moon before anyone ever tried going there, and I wondered whether it would ever be accomplished in my lifetime. During the years of the space program, I was still a boy, but the astronauts were my heroes. I marveled at how they trained, how they were able to withstand multiple forces of gravity in a test centrifuge that simulated conditions of blasting off in the nose cone of a rocket ship into space. Later, especially after the movie of the same name, it was common to refer to the qualities these men possessed as, "The Right Stuff," and it wasn't just about their physical capabilities but their mental make-up as well.

As I was nearing the age when I might have qualified in some way for astronaut training, the space program was put in mothballs, so to speak. Due to the total saturation of numerous trips to the moon, public interest in matters pertaining to space waned in the mind of the general public, and as a result, there was a decreased national budget for space exploration. Still, I collected images of the moon including proof of landings there. I especially loved the photographs taken through telescopes showing the tracks made by vehicles on the lunar surface. I hated anyone who believed the landings were some sort of conspiracy, that they were faked, and I unloaded arguments on them, deadly accurate in showing how idiotic and lame-brained their ignorant positions were, even if they went away pretending they were not convinced.

I also followed the Voyager missions closely and marveled at the pictures of the planets sent back, and I put on my 3D glasses and admired the first pictures of the martian landscape as taken by the Mars Rover. I instantly felt like I was standing there on the red planet, still at home in every way with the idea of going into space.

So when I hear about the new lunar program, I immediately hired a personal trainer and began to work out, putting myself into the best physical shape possible. I also read books on increasing my mental awareness and calmness under pressure, which to me was more like reactivating old machinery, dusting off *the right stuff* that already made up the console of my mind.

Soon the day of applying was at hand. I figured I was ready for what I expected would be stiff competition, and happily, I got out of bed feeling I was at my best. I could run a mile in just over four minutes, do five hundred push-ups, six hundred sit-ups and press double my weight. For my age, this was amazing, but I knew the space agency wouldn't be as concerned about age at this point. I'd seen that when older astronauts were given second chances in space on shuttle missions, and they were even older than me and in worse shape.

But when I make my appearance to apply for the program, what I thought was the waiting room is filled with people on crutches and in wheelchairs. I think I must be in the hospital portion of the building, in the emergency waiting room perhaps. Then a nurse asks me if she can help me, and when I say I am there for the lunar mission evaluation, there is a gasp in the room as if people can't believe their ears. "How dare you come in here like this!" snaps the nurse. "These brave and good pioneers here will benefit from the lesser gravity of the moon in this new program. They'll find it easier to deal with their handicaps, but you have no business in here. Are you seriously trying to horn in on their opportunity? You should be ashamed of yourself!"

Spring Thaw

I am a great baseball player on a mediocre team, and in an effort to save my talents for the next year, management decides to "shut me down," which means to not play me for the duration of the season. This seems to work rather well for me as the next Spring I pick it up where I left off, and again, late in the season when we are out of contention, they suggest shutting me down again. But I have a better idea. I explain that pretty much baseball is my entire life. I have no other interests, and nothing else going at the time, so why not do that cryogenic thing and freeze me? This would not only "shut me down" for next season, but it would basically extend my baseball life, so to speak, adding six months of life to every year I play, so that if I were to be expected to play ball another twenty years, I would easily play at least another ten on top of that.

So they think it over and agree that they would probably get more playing time out of me in the long run, so they put me into cryogenic suspension. When Spring comes and they thaw me out, I find I'm a little tired, then reason that I'm still at the point where they shut me down and just need a little rest. So I start a month late, which is great for me, but the team has fallen behind in the standings already, and we never make it up.

So the next Fall, they "shut me down" earlier, but they don't freeze me for a month to give me ample time to rest so that when they thaw me out in the Spring, I'll be ready to play. But when they wake me up in the Spring, they have some bad news. Apparently some of the people in charge of the cryogenic freezer units got drunk one night, cut my head off and played ball with it. They were fired, and doctors were able to reattach my head, and because it was frozen, there is not so much damage, just some bruising that will take some time to go away. But there was one crack in the skull that they repaired with some uncertainty whether there will be any side effects until I get back to playing. They tell me everything to fulfill the requirements of full disclosure, and after hearing it, I agree to try to play despite the situation and possible new risk factors.

When the day comes, I realize instantly that there's a problem because I can't lay off the high fast ball. I start striking out every time

I'm up, and I'm forced to retire from baseball early after further tests reveal that the damage done to me in and around the freezer will take thirty years off my life.

End Game

I'm looking out the window one day, and I notice my neighbor is busy harvesting, gathering things and building what looks like some kind of container or bomb shelter on stilts, and he's putting everything inside it. I head outside and ask what he's doing, and he replies very out of breath and talking very fast that I better get started on mine. "Started on my what?" I ask him. And he tells me it's his endgame, the passage to the next life, strong enough to endure the last days of this one.

And he gets very agitated and explains how his religion and experiences are laced through the structure to give it strength, and how the construction of such a structure is part of life, how everyone needs to do it, that in the end it becomes what life is all about, that you'll find yourself lying in bed one day, about to die, with no where to go if you don't have yours ready, that it's a terrible end unless one builds the passage to the endgame and employs all the power of one's mind, all the integrity of one's beliefs to make it right. But by the end when you're old and have no sense of the answer, that having known it here and now at the top of your form, that this is the time to do it, to take advantage of it and secure a place in the next world by having a plan, executing it and making the passage.

Then as he catches his breath, he apologizes and says he's got to get on with the work, so much to do, and that again, I'd better get started on mine because if I wait too long, it will just be too late. So I head back inside a bit perplexed and keep looking out the window as he goes about his construction project. I wonder if I should have asked him if he needed any help, but there was something strangely single-minded and crazed about the whole thing, that I knew in advance he would say that he had to do it by himself.

The work area around the structure looks like a disaster, but it appears the building itself is taking shape nicely, and I find myself wondering what an endgame is and whether or not there's really anything to what he's doing. A few days later, while sitting on my couch, I hear a loud noise outside and look to see smoke coming from the structure and my neighbor on the ground below it between the stilts. I rush out and find him dead, and as I look at him and the structure, I can tell that it's as if he had been spit out of the thing like there was some kind of malfunction, but I also know it was something spiritual and philosophical as the inside of the structure is a wreck, and it is then I realized the onus is on me, that the same thing will happen to me if I don't build mine right.

In the Dungeon

I am a king in the Middle Ages where I have a castle with not just a moat, but many other security measures in place because I have many enemies, and over the years they have tried to kill me many times. It seems that everything I try to do to defend myself, they are hard at work devising something to undo me despite the protection. I built a higher, thicker wall, and they built higher, stronger ladders. I made the windows too thin for arrows to pass through, and they made their arrows thinner so as to slip them through.

I also know that they have designed schemes that they have yet to try because I do not give them the chance. I know, for example, that they have perfected a catapult that is deadly accurate at a distance of ten miles. Were I to even stand for a few minutes in the same place, I have no doubt it would be the end of me. I calculated how long it would take for a missile to arrive, and I just move accordingly at brief intervals so they will not shoot this secret weapon from afar. But of course they have traditional archers at the ready nearby. But then I have a suit of armor they cannot pierce. However, given the history, I am even now fortifying my armor since I am certain they're in the process of improving their arrowheads to penetrate all of the armor that I'm wearing.

As it stands, I spend much of my time in the dungeon because it is the safest place in the castle for me. I know they may try to tunnel under the moat, but when the castle was built decades ago, I made sure the foundations went down hundreds of feet, and there are many traps down there, and to get from any point in the foundation up to the dungeon is, quite frankly, impossible. But being down here all day every day affects my ability to rule well, I'm afraid, or at least it did for a number of years.

Whenever I was down here for more than a few days, I would get depressed and snap at somebody. Now it seems I am fully acclimated, but it is like having turned to stone in some ways. I don't much laugh or cry, just carry out my rule in a castle generally under siege at all times. I suppose this is the mature way to do it. One might say I'm at my best, seasoned by many years of experience and hardened by a constant war. But such a life has a tendency to lead to a nickname like "The Hammer" or "The Lionhearted," and I really don't want to be reduced to a simple phrase even though my whole life has been reduced to a very simple and singular purpose, which is the survival of my rule against the enemy that does not wish merely to kill me, but to wipe me out entirely, to erase my ideas permanently from the face of the earth and to leave my castle in ruins in the process.

I used to revel in it, but now it's making me tired. What can people learn from a few rocks and broken walls anyway? I can imagine time doing that one day, but I cannot let my enemies be the cause. In my daydreams I imagine calling them to a conference, and as they gather around the castle, the walls drop on them. And without them, we have a great patio, an open castle until they gain a new force, at which point I have the walls pulled up again. If I could manage something like that in the springtime, it would at least be a good way to get out of the dungeon for a while and smell the roses.

Family Plague

There's a strange plague going around, and when I discover its symptoms and long-term effects, I'm at least consoled by the fact that it is not life-threatening. But when I see the effect it's having on people, I start doing everything I can to avoid catching it. I try to stay away from everyone. But I have to continue to work, so I wash my hands often, keeping them away from my face, and I don't go into the public except when absolutely necessary. I do not take trains and wait until after the sidewalks have cleared before walking home, as it can get rather crowded during rush hour.

Every day it seems more and more people are becoming victims of this plague. Today I was sitting at my desk, and the woman in the office across the hall from mine started crying. First she let out a scream, which I believe is when she realized she was a victim. But when I got up and looked in her office, I saw she wasn't crying. It was coming from under her blouse, and I knew she had the plague.

This plague is really quite awful as the faces of one's deceased relatives begin to come out of the abdomen or back as well as other places on the victim. The dead come back to life and basically won't shut up. They talk to the victims. They make demands. They tell the victim what to do.

In the case of the woman across the hall from me, her mother was always pretty much a weeper when she was alive, and this poor girl was actually set free in a way by her mother's passing. Now she has her permanently on her belly, crying at just about everything, and what's worse, now her daughter can't hide anything from her.

I'm afraid she might kill herself, so I call for an ambulance but they are so busy they are ignoring calls at this point. I've seen many people with multiple protrusions, whole families and several generations of faces all vying for attention, calling out for the shirt to be removed so they can see, shouting to stop sitting back on their faces in the chair. It's horrible, and I wonder how it happens except that people do get into us, and into those that get into us, so in a way they're always there. But to have them appear like this is terrible.

Then it finally happens to me. My parents, who were divorced and died within a few years of one another many years ago appear on my stomach and start fighting. "Shut up! Shut up! SHUT UP!" I yell, and I hear the woman across the hall telling her mother who has started crying again that she shouldn't cry because I wasn't talking to her.

Promise of Life

My father always used to tell me the story of when I was born, how I almost died, and how he held my little hand in the incubator and kept saying, "You're going to live. You're going to live," and how I responded to his words like I knew he was there. And through my childhood, he was always there, and whenever I was sick with the flu, he would take my temperature, administer medicine and drive out to the store for anything else I needed even in the middle of the night, throwing in a gift or two to help make me feel better, and he'd always tell me not to worry, that I was going to live.

I'm not sure when it started to happen, but those words, that mantra, began to have the opposite effect on me. I wasn't really all that worried while sick that anything serious would happen to me. It almost seemed like it really worried my father though, more than me. Considering what he'd been through with my having been premature, all those days and nights in the hospital and me being his only child, one can understand his getting a little bit jumpy when I wasn't feeling well. His reminding me that I was going to live seemed like an effort to convince himself, to drive out negative thoughts, but at some point it was like those negative thoughts came into me, and I started thinking about the fact that someday I was going to die.

I didn't like the thought of it at all. It was a horrible thing to think about, but it isn't hard to realize there was a world before I was born. It's just harder to think of not being here forever. A sense of nothingness is a difficult state of mind to establish. Once it began to infect me, the thought stood high in the sky like a distant cloud. I could never tell how far away big clouds are, and I could only say of this one that it was coming someday. So I thought a lot about death, about not being here, and I think it made me more introverted than my father would have liked.

Even when I was little, he wanted to take me out to play sports with him. My mother used to say kiddingly that when I was born my father brought out the mitts to play catch. I enjoyed it, and I liked learning about the various games. When it came time to participate, my father even coached my teams. He was very active on the sidelines cheering us on, and he was very generous with the other boys, but I was the only one to whom he would say, "You're going to live," when I got hurt running the base paths or defending the goal playing soccer. It always made me think the opposite again, that I was going to die.

By the time I got into high school, my father was encouraging me to go out for the school teams, but I wasn't that interested in sports anymore. There was something about the competition that I no longer liked. I thought competition and the need to win brought out the worst in people, while my father always argued it brought out the best in them. When I did watch games, I enjoyed them more at the beginning of the season or when the team was out of contention. I felt closer to heaven when I wasn't concerned about the score. It did not matter to me. I hated what people did when they had to win at all costs. I hated how professional athletes cheated, made themselves monsters with chemicals to make more money, and they didn't care what people thought of them. While my father wanted me to watch the games with him, to be a fan like he was, I wanted to do other things like work on my bike, and later my car. I've always enjoyed anything that could make me move faster than my legs, and as soon as I got my license to drive, the first thing I did was get two speeding tickets, which rather infuriated my father. But after the first one, he didn't take away my license but told me to keep driving, that the second one would cause the state to take it from me. The psychology would have been valid for most people, and I did slow down for a while, but when I got the second ticket, my father did call a lawyer friend who helped me get out of it, so I ended up on probation and able to keep my license. But something about that whole affair made my father a little distant, like he started thinking about the real dangers I was facing, bringing on myself. He really started warning me about accidents and what happens to kids who drive drunk. I hated hearing it, but I noticed he stopped saying, "You're going to live."

When I went away to college, I sort of lost touch with him. We'd talk on the phone a bit now and then, and he always encouraged me to do my best, but I always thought he was somewhat disappointed in my choices, that I wasn't more like him. But I worried about him, probably with better reason because during the twenty or so years that he was watching me get stronger, I was watching him slowly turn gray. He slouched something terrible, a habit he picked up from the way he sat on the couch watching games. Anyway, his health was a greater concern to me the older he got. Still, I thought he might out-live me because he didn't smoke or drink, and his father and grand-father both lived into their nineties.

But one day I got the dreaded call from my mother to come home, that he was in the hospital with a terrible pneumonia. I got there as fast as I could, and I was able to talk with him a while. The game was on television, and while I sat there, he mostly watched it, so the topic was about what was happening on the field. Then, at one point he reached for my hand, which I gave him, and he said to me, "You're going to die, aren't you?" To which I answered, "Yes, some day," and his response was, "That's what I thought," at which he turned his head away from me and watched the rest of the game quietly before going to sleep. He died the next day, and I kept wishing that I had replied, "No Dad, I'm going to live. I'm going to live." That's what he really wanted to hear, and I'm certain it would have made a big difference if I'd said it.

Looking for Answers

I don't understand anything or have any of the answers, but I do have lots of friends. I was also blessed with good looks and a great sense of humor, so all is not lost. The opposite gender is very attentive, and while I don't understand anything or have any of the answers, for the most part, there is something very comfortable about my life, and generally I would classify most of my feelings and emotions as falling under the heading, "Happiness."

But I don't even understand why that should be the case. When I do the math, it doesn't add up that I could be happy without understanding anything or having any of the answers. This anomaly begins to bother me so I go to the library and start looking through philosophy and religion books for the meaning of life. There is such a variety of ideas, many of them contradictory to one another, that my head starts spinning. There are whole nations following one idea while other nations believe something else, and yet they are often so opposite one another that both cannot be true.

In some ways it seems obvious that certain ideas are false, but this doesn't seem to matter to those who believe them. They obviously don't pursue the truth in the sense that it matters whether their beliefs are valid. It almost seems that belief offers its own inner form of validation. After perusing many books, in some ways I understand even less than before and have fewer answers, but in another way I'm understanding more and feel I might be getting closer to an answer.

It matters now that I continue with my research at all costs. I start canceling dinner dates with my friends, and I also stop dating. I believe when I get closer to the truth, I'll be ready to socialize again, even better off than before, more suited to being the kind of person I should be, not confused and clueless, and with much to share. I even have reason to hope that people will like me more. I continue reading and become well-versed in many ideologies.

I can explain them through and through, even point out one bit of error in the logic that throws off a whole system, leading to crimes of reason, genocide. Soon I reach the point that I feel I understand everything, that I have all the answers, but perhaps I only believe this is the case, and my beliefs are getting the best of me. When I try to make inroads back with my friends, I find they are unreceptive. In fact they want nothing to do with me. "Take a look at yourself," one of them says, and I think it is about my attitude, that my new knowledge must make me seem a bit arrogant, but when I look in the mirror I realize that they were talking literally. Somehow during all of my studies I had grown shabby and hunched over. I am very ugly not to mention very unhappy.

Corn Fest

The day of my "Corn Fest" has arrived, and I am more than a bit apprehensive as it means all the people in my life will be coming together where the focus will be on me, and of course, the corn harvest. Will it be a good one? I mean, will the corn be good is a huge question and has a bearing on the judgement of one's entire life. Even though most of my life has been lived, it could be a great thing going forward to have further backing and support from friends and family rendered extremely positive by good corn. On the other hand, I've seen Corn Fests go the other way many a time. When the corn is bad, people literally abandon their family members, treating them as if it had just been learned that they have the plague. One can worry about it all one wants, but when the Corn Fest comes, it all goes from imaginary to real.

As my Corn Fest begins, it is just as I feared. Everyone has come with all the elements of life, their excuses, their problems and doubts, their failures, goiter problems, their friends' funerals, and their endless discussion and boring details of what happened during their own Corn Fests.

Then there are the bugs and the heat. It isn't enough that the humidity is high. My table has to be situated close to the pots of boiling corn so the steam can waft over me and clean out my pores. Some old woman, a great aunt of some kind, tells me it is good luck, and she adds that judging by the smell of the corn, this is going to be a good batch, as she recalls back in '44 when her dying father had his Corn Fest, that not only was the corn the best it ever was, but famous doctors received recommendations and took on his case, and though he died, they revived him, after which he lived another 30 years.

All I can think is how many Corn Fests that adds up to for her. I can't even count how many I've attended, and I see everyone is here, including the Corn Fest untouchables, relatives of mine who at some point had a bad Corn Fest such that nobody talks to them now, though they talk amongst themselves, and it always appears they are actually having the best time. Sometimes I wish I were one of them, but the good-time thing seems only to apply to Corn Fests. The rest of the time, the untouchables are miserable.

Meanwhile I have to stand here in the receiving line and listen to person after person telling me their problems like I am some kind of priest in a confessional, able to absolve them, forgive them, fix them, all with the power of the corn. It all makes me wonder, if it's such a cleansing, why didn't all their problems get taken care of during their Corn Fest?

Then, finally, the moment of truth comes, and the corn is served. Great heaps of butter and plenty of salt later, we're all amazed at how good it is. I'm on about my 10th ear, receiving envelopes filled with money, already too many to carry, when someone slaps me on the back while I'm swallowing, causing me to choke and throw up corn all over the place.

Unfortunately, whatever the cause, this sadly signifies to everyone that the corn is actually bad, and it negates everything I have accrued so far. The guest of honor does not spit up at a Corn Fest without repercussions. It is a terrible and outrageous turn of events, and I turn around and see it is my brother who had slapped me on the back. He is smirking, putting his thumb up, and I realize he did it to me on purpose, hoping everything would go wrong for me. Nobody seems to suspect there was any ill-will in his congratulatory backslap, but it wouldn't matter anyway. The results are in, and they can't be changed. In any case, I know he did it because he has always been jealous, and I may be untouchable, but it doesn't mean I can't do something in return. It's a terrible outcome for me personally, but all in all, it's just your average Corn Fest.

War Strategies

I am a consultant for the military listening in on invasion plans for what will be a total war. I'm just sitting there doodling while presentation after presentation describes the casualties to be expected per type of ordinance used, that sort of thing, when something strange about the plan spurs me into raising my hand. I ask the general who happens to be speaking to go over a point again, and looking a bit irritated at having to repeat himself, he reiterates that as the battle progresses, all the flies being generated by the dead will be collected and concentrated as a weapon against enemy survivors as a means of subduing them by a supremely tortuous diversion.

To this I respond that flies tend to bring out the killer instinct in all of us, that whenever a fly happens to come through an open door or window in my house, I immediately go into battle mode, grabbing a newspaper section and rolling it up, using lights to drive it into the smallest room, so that confined it is easier to kill. The general replies that this is the point, that the enemy will be distracted. But then I point out that when butterflies are introduced, we all stand back in admiration and silent deference to watch them and allow them to continue on their fluttery journeys.

So the military takes my consultation into consideration and conducts a test on groups of soldiers, and indeed, those subjected to flies go into a frenzy, waving at them, which ultimately makes them battle ready and difficult to defeat; while those over whom the butterflies are released put down their guns and hold out their fingers, quietly standing still allowing these insects to land on them, the more the better, which makes the soldiers peaceful but easy targets if you were going to be shooting at them.

But given the results of these tests, I submit that there could be peace as a result, that the test subjects disarmed themselves and were filled with a natural reverence for life, which would lead to good results in peace talks; while exposure to flies brought out every negative feeling one had against what is vile and revolting in life, causing that test group to stand firm against them, ready to fight to the death the same as each of us grabs a swatter once we find a fly in our house.

But the generals are concerned with the whole idea, and ask that butterflies be released on them, to which they respond by killing every last one of them. "But this is ridiculous," I tell them. "You were not responding honestly and knew you were furthering your own agenda. This renders the test invalid."

The generals disagree and have me removed. As I am taken away in handcuffs, they are discussing whether it is possible to put poisonous stingers on butterflies, or what else could make them deadly. As they continue with their plans for total war, I am put in a cell near the latrines where the flies give me no peace.

Parasite

I have what looks like some kind of insect bite on my arm that I respond to in the typical way by scratching it until I realize that it doesn't help, then I apply some anti-itch cream and ignore it as best as I can. The medicine seems to do its job, and I forget about the bite until someone asks me, "What the heck is that on your arm?"

When I look, I'm as shocked as they are to see a pretty large festering sore that only a few hours previously was a small bump. Immediately I am aware of the sensations it brings, both pain and itching that I hadn't noticed as I have been totally engrossed in something else.

But now this grabs all my attention as I can see it is getting bigger by the hour. By now it is evening, and I call my doctor's answering service. By the time he calls me back, the thing is as big as a baseball. He tells me to go to the emergency room at the hospital, and to not do anything to it, suggesting it may have been some kind of reaction to the cream, which I have used many times before without problem.

By the time I get to the hospital, rather than take me right in, the attendant informs me I am not up to date on my medical insurance, and by the time it is all straightened out, the whole left side of my body is engulfed.

When I go into the examination room, a whole team of doctors meets me, everyone except my own doctor who apparently was too busy to respond. I hear the doctors say they've never seen anything like it, or anything that worsened at such a rate. Now my entire body is covered with some kind of infection, a red, pus-leaking blistering rash. One of the doctors asks where the original sore was which is quite obvious as it's become a huge, rounded boil about the size of a football. He begins to probe and cut it open, and to his astonishment, he finds a very small, completely-accurate-in-every-detail miniature version of me inside.

This doctor suggests the sore was a kind of womb or incubator for an amazing transformation. My body is now looking like the giant version of a despicable bug with biting fangs, something that might have bitten me in the first place, they surmise. The doctors suggest there has been a transference of survival that will save me. The new version of me is growing faster, and I am going fast. I know it didn't get my soul, I still feel I have that, but it looks and acts like me. They see the miniature version of me is growing fast. They think it is me. But it's not, yet now I can't speak.

Now my other self is full size and thanking the doctors. He is looking back at me with a smirk. I cannot move, and the doctors declare it is time to get rid of the awful carcass to make room for the next patient.

The Melon

I am seated at a small table on which rests a large bowl of the most perfectly ripened and delectable melon I have ever seen in my life. It is gorgeous in color and fresh in fragrance. As I pick up a slice and hold it between my fingers, my lightest touch, which is just enough to keep from dropping it, is still more than enough pressure to begin to force juices to flow from within it. As I place it in my mouth and take a bite, my whole mouth fills with an indescribably fabulous taste, and again those juices just run down my chin.

I use a napkin to clean up, and I just have to laugh that this is just the most scrumptious and healthy thing I have ever seen or tasted. It puts me in mind of a time long ago when such melons were the pride of an island nation somewhere. I imagine someone on this island centuries ago stumbling upon a small melon patch growing in the wild. After the wonderful smell captivates him, he tastes one and is overwhelmed with joy with the discovery. He brings samples back, and soon the people are farming the melons, even making it central to their religious ceremonies over the centuries.

I take another bite and think at some point a visitor on a ship happens to anchor there, where he is welcomed by the inhabitants and treated to a fine meal including one of the forebears of the melon that now sits before me. When that man leaves, he goes back to his own country with some gifts, and when he presents a few melons to his king, the council is brought in for a taste, after which they quickly decide to go to war and invade this small island nation to gobble up, or in more official wording, to take control of the melons.

I take another bite, and another whole swath of history unfolds before my eyes. I see huge plantations of the sweet fruit, rows and rows tended by slaves who once had owned the land. I see the conquerors whipping them if so much as one melon is dropped and broken. I see suffering and pain. I take yet another bite and see a man with some seeds trying to get the melons to grow somewhere else. The experiment fails miserably. I see more wars over the island, and so many deaths over the centuries that in some ways only the precious melon itself is a survivor, needing nobody to tend it in its natural state, and yet once discovered, no one seems to be able to live without it. It was, even for me, the first thing I thought of, a "must have" for this occasion. What more could a man want to put him in mind of what it means to live? But at the same time, it changes people. Even as I love it, even as we all love it, (where if we all collaborated, there could be enough for everyone), I feel surrounded by people who begrudge it to me; and yet because of it, I feel more human, closer to everyone, a changed man in another sense.

Suddenly I hear the sound of a key and my voyage through history ends as time runs out for me. I hear a guard say, "Dead Man Walking," and as I am made to stand up before finishing my last meal, I reach down to grab one last slice of the delectable fruit, but it is so juicy it slips between my fingers and splashes on the floor.

An Unwelcome Visitor

I am in a perfect town, not so much as a citizen but more as an observer, curious about how it came to be recognized and projected as being without fault of any kind; a claim that I find ridiculous on the face of it. Looking back at my journey, it was rather a bumpy ride getting here, but actually as soon as I crossed the village borders, it was very smooth, and if I could find fault, I might have to say it was with the car in which I rode, and nothing to do with the road itself. Looking closely at it, even with a magnifying glass down on my hands and knees, each small pebble actually seems to fit with the next one like patio paving stones. I'm not sure what kind of process they used to lay it down, but I would think it would be very costly and take years to do even 20 feet of a two-lane highway like that, but I could see it holding up very well indeed.

If I'm going to be critical, then I'm off to a bad start. I walk down the main street and begin my examination of the people, and immediately I find plenty to complain about. I wouldn't use the word obese, but I see there are some rather large people. The clothes they're wearing are interesting. The fabric seems familiar like something I saw once in a science program about things that don't wear out. I guess that it's considered fashionable to call your village perfect just because you have a few instances where technology has set you a little bit ahead of other places.

I notice rain clouds coming over and that nobody seems bothered by the thunder. Then I see a dome begin to rise and cover the town. My visitor brochure explains that the rain water will be collected and purified to perfection, then used in every imaginable way to better the lives of the villagers.

So I ask myself, how can you make lives better if they're already perfect? Then a policeman approaches and says it's time for me to leave, which is a red flag, a huge flaw in their legal system. "Why should I leave?" I ask. "You're making a mess," he tells me. I'm leaving a trail of filth. I look back and see they're hosing down visible footprints I've made on their "streets of gold." My breath, he says, is so bad it's killing him. "Well la tee da! And hoity toity to you too," I say to him, as men in gleaming hazmat suits ride up in a beautiful, silent, streamlined city vehicle and drive me to my car waiting just beyond the village limits.

After being in the quiet town for only a short time, I'm surprised how embarrassed I feel to hear my engine sputtering so loudly as I start it up, and for the first time I notice how terrible the exhaust of my car smells. In a strange way, much as I hate them all, I really want to stay, but as I depart, they sneer, "Don't come back," which is perfectly rude.

But I don't want to go back, except to go shopping, maybe. There were a few things I wanted to buy. As I get home, I keep thinking about that place. I feel a need to get back, so I get my best clothes and brush my teeth, but they obviously have tracking devices that sense my approach, and at a short distance from the village, they come out to stop me. No matter what I do, they won't let me back in. I camp outside the dome waiting for a chance, which is when I realize there's a whole community of people like myself out here trying to get in. We circle the dome, peering in the glass or whatever it is, a pure substance that doesn't smear or smudge, and we also stand as proof that nobody's perfect, but also as unhappy witnesses to the fact that we believe perfection does exist.

Rite of Passage

Concerned that the rites of passage have been all but eliminated from modern life despite being an essential experience for a boy in becoming a man, I decide to manufacture such a life-changing or life-transitioning event for my son and begin by consulting books on how I might best go about achieving the best results. Being that many rites of passage are grounded in some kind of religious mythology relevant to a specific society or tribe, much of it seems foreign or irrelevant to me, or at least not applicable, though there are certain compelling elements that I feel could be adapted and incorporated into whatever I do. The one I like the best is where the men take the boy by a kind of mock force, and the mother who is "in on it" holds him when he runs to her for protection in such a way that he feels supported by her, though in the end he is unable to ward off their stronger attack, so she lets him go.

I decide a fishing trip would be a good scenario, and I work my wife into the picture by giving my son so many jobs to do that eventually he goes to complain to her. She is supposed to push him back to me, but in fact he makes such a convincing argument, such a show of emotion, that she decides to side with him, and I end up packing the car while she makes him cookies and milk and packs him some banana bread for the ride. I get nothing but what I bring myself, some cheese sandwiches, a thermos of coffee and some beer for when I get to the national forest. There I have already selected a pristine lake in the far north, and my plan is to tip the boat over and feign unconsciousness and have my son save me. This will all be relatively easy for him as the life jackets are very hefty. All he'll have to do is paddle and push me to shore, and I don't plan to do this in deep water but maybe ten feet out from shore. When the moment comes, and I stand in the boat, shifting my weight heavily to one side, I cannot flip the boat for some reason, and I consider it may be too much for him after all.

So instead I pretend to accidentally fall in the water and act unconscious, but when I start to float, he does nothing and says nothing. When finally I open an eye, he asks if I want a sandwich. At 14 years old he's actually more sly than I gave him credit for, so while trying to think of what else I may do, we just sit there fishing. Suddenly he hooks what has to be one of the biggest muskies I've ever seen, fights it for nearly an hour before finally pulling it in. Looking at the magnificent fish, a possible state record, he says, "I think I want to let it go," and I realize that letting my son off the hook was equally the right choice for me. I believe the trip itself still manages to do the job of granting my son passage, in many ways because of the fundamental tie in of the spirit to nature and the fact that he respected my effort to try to make it more exciting though it turned out to be plenty interesting on its own. What really floored me was how he told my wife when we got home that he had to give me mouth-to-mouth resuscitation as I fell out of a boat and hit my head on a rock. I still had a bump on my head, but as far as I knew, it never happened, but he told the story so convincingly, adding that I'd had a memory loss, that I'm planning to stay in bed for a few days, hoping I'll make it through this experience without permanent issues.

The Line

I'm standing in line with everyone when word comes down the line that someone stepped out. The news causes ripples, buzzing along as people wonder how it happened. Everyone wants to know whether someone stepped out or maybe fell. They want to know if they were pushed by someone else, and if so, who might have done the pushing. There are lots of famous people somewhere in line, too far away to even begin to think it might be possible to stand near them or brush shoulders, but on nearby televisions, they drone on and on with white straight teeth and smiles about the benefits of standing together, how it is the right thing to do, and everyone needs to do it. But every so often, even one of these actors steps out, which is big news that comes down the line very quickly.

Quite often there is news of apologies for stepping out, and people say they are back, but it is common for these incidents to haunt and follow someone the rest of their lives. Everyone keeps a kind of mental record of such incidents because there are rules that should not be broken. Most of us keep our minds on that, our focus on going wherever everyone else is going, as being in line not knowing where you're going is far better than falling out. As long as I've stood here, it's strange, but the camera has never been on me for some reason, and not even on the many miles where I'm standing. Each day there are constant reports updating the line, but it seems there's a bias for the front not the back, and of course, great interest on those who stepped out.

What's also interesting is that many who are accused deny it. Even with video evidence, they claim a kind of narrow position that staying is particularly a matter of attitude, of what's inside, and that as long as one is "in-line" in that regard, one can never be accused of stepping out. But this is sidestepping the issue. In its own way, it represents a kind of falling out, which really cannot be tolerated since we must hold the line against the other lines being drawn, like those all around the world that oppose our method of lining up. We even have a special way to line up against those who oppose us. We have harsh penalties for those who fall out, or won't get into line during those times.

But I've always been one to stand with others, and I've taught my children to do the same. So many generations of my family have stayed in line that we have made it a kind of trench in which we walk, and quite frankly, it is so deep we would have to actually climb up over it and not even begin to be able to step out.

At least that is what I thought, but in the end, a rumor reaches me, rippling down the line, that I have stepped out. It is not unusual for such things to happen, and normally all one needs to do is show that he is in line, but in my case I've been in line so long that it is considered being out of line, a ridiculous assertion I say, but somehow it is backed up by the fact that my trench has gotten so deep that I cannot be seen, not even my head. So they come and pour dirt in the trench, burying me, and the line fills the gap, and the lesson is presented that once in a while it is important to step out of line if only to shift focus, shake off the dirt, start another path along proper lines, so as to not bury oneself in the old ways.

The Blur

I am with my beloved grandmother as she is passing, and she is so brave and taking it all in so well without pain killers of any kind, all with a clear mind, and I ask her how she is able to do it, and she answers, "I learned to trust the blur." I'm not really sure what she means, and before I can ask her to elaborate, the doctor comes in and basically dispatches me so he can check up on her in privacy. It turns out sadly to be the last time I ever speak with her, and when I bring up her last words to see what people think she meant, I get a wide range of answers.

Most seem to think that because she was so close to death, she was probably not lucid, even if what she said seemed compelling. My mother believed that it was about my grandmother's eyes being bad her whole life, where even a current prescription for lenses she was wearing would have gone blurry on her, and she had learned to live with not seeing well. But for me, the way she said she trusted the blur indicated a situation she was guided by, not a literal situation she was just comfortable with. I asked her about dealing with death, so a general statement on the condition of her eyes was a non-sequitur. In the end, I probably side with those who saw it as a cryptic, mysterious remark, one of those strangely meaningful gems typically quipped when one is slipping away.

But I always keep that thought her comment generated, that inspiration with me as a kind of mantra, a guiding light in the darkness or fog, if you will, which is particularly appropriate for me in my line of work as I operate one of the ferries that sails daily between Hyannis and Nantucket, Massachusetts, and there's often quite a bit of fog and mist. Even with all the instruments including GPS, I still have to rely on my instincts and trust the blur, so to speak, which for me is when I see a kind of gray in the mist that I know will be the shoreline.

I have just learned to recognize and trust its shape, and every time I see it on my approach, when nobody else can tell where we are, I surprise them all by declaring, "Land Ho!" and within minutes it all comes clear. Some say that it's no big deal because I've made the trip so many times, my inner clock tells me when I'm getting close, but I know it's more than that. It's instinctive.

On one trip though, I find myself becoming very ill on my way back from the island, and by the time the boat docks, an ambulance is waiting for me. I couldn't help remembering how misty and blurry the day was both ways all the way, and when the doctor tells me a few days later after all the tests come back that I only have a few months to live, I am shaken to the core.

For whatever reason, I never spent any time in matters pertaining to the voyage of the soul, on where it goes into the mist, into the unknown, and I become frantic and lost, uncontrollably emotional day in and day out. Everyone reminds me of how badly I am taking everything, and of what my grandmother said, reminding me how bravely she went out; and though I thought I understood another possible meaning to what she said to me that no one mentioned in our discussions, and though I thought I was living it as well, I realized it was all lost on me as the only thing I feel myself is fear and distrust going into the blur.

Guardian Angel

I am an angel whose job it is to watch over my delegated share of living souls as their appointed guardian and play my harp at what would be considered key moments in which one soul is at stake, and by playing effectively get that person back on track without his realizing that his guardian angel played a huge part in his sudden turnaround. I do this successfully for a long time, and I'm highly regarded by my fellow angels. I don't know how many people I've managed to help, but it's quite a few obviously because sooner or later everyone needs outside intervention of some kind, and there's nothing quite so effective as the heavenly variety.

But one day while I am hovering over a parking lot about to play my harp to stop one of my flock from making the huge mistake of meeting someone in a motel room, something very strange happens. The music I play sounds terrible like the harp is out of tune. As a result, the man I was trying to help behaves irrationally according to the bad music of the spheres and gets back in his car and drives over a cliff. A heavenly assembly is called where I am made to apologize to this poor soul now in the heavenly chorus, which is no problem because I truly am sorry. But I still do not understand what happened.

It turns out from the inquiry that some of the strings from my harp were missing, and what is worse, certain people, also members of the flock I was assigned to protect, are found tied up with the strings from my harp, *after* they did things that my music was supposed to prevent them from doing. They were not killed, but their own acts did still condemn them.

In any case, all these matters make for tough judgements, which are the very things that I am there to prevent. What's worse, a closer review of the past reveals that it was me who tied them up, but I have no recollection of this, and further inquiry suggests that to do all this I must have a spiritual disorder that has polarized my identity, a drop of evil in the mix as they say. But I defend myself and declare if I had done it, then it must have been a kind of sleepwalking, which they wave off because angels do not sleep. They seem to all think they know what happened even though I'm confused, but they don't take my honest purity into account, and so I'm condemned, to be dispensed with, in the first grand celestial execution of its kind, to walk a plank in the center of the galaxy that will drop me into a black hole.

"Where is my guardian angel?" I keep crying as the other angels, my former friends, prod me toward my downfall from grace. At that moment, there is a message that a spirit that looks exactly like me has been seen operating in my district, tying up people while I was on trial. The likeness is so perfect that everyone says it is me, except it is not. It has strings all around its neck ready for use in tying people up, and when questioned, he disappears in a puff of greasy black smoke, a sure sign that this doppelganger is from hell, which vindicates me, and at the last moment I am reprieved. Despite this wonderful news, for some reason after that, none of the other angels really treats me the way they used to. My interpretation is that it is a case of eternal guilty conscience.

Home Run

I'm walking my dog along a path in a city park on what is a beautiful, clear and blue, early autumn day when my dog suddenly lunges at a baseball that unexpectedly rolls past us at a brisk speed. He pulls me off balance for a moment, but the leash holds, and I look back and watch the ball rolling quickly toward the street. A few moments later, a man runs by us, clearly chasing after the ball, and I look in the direction from which he is running, and I see a baseball field ahead of me full of players looking my way, shouting and lining up in expectation of a play once the ball is thrown back.

There is also a man in a baseball helmet already rounding second base, obviously the one who hit the ball, and as I look back at the outfielder still chasing it, I say to myself, "Home run," and continue walking the dog.

As we approach the field, the cheers from the long ball have yet to subside as it turns out the homer won the game. It is quite a celebration as we approach. The winded outfielder is walking slowly back to the bench, his head down, and my dog is pulling the leash to try to get to other dogs being walked by their masters.

As I reach the backstop, I stop at the drinking fountain behind it, and while getting a drink, I hear a voice behind me saying, "Did you see that?"

I look up, and I see a friend of mine several feet up the backstop, which is made of interlaced storm fencing. His shoes are nestled in the fence, his toes sticking through, his fingers laced above him as well, and he's grinning at me. It is a huge smile, which indicates to me that whatever it was he's talking about, I would remember if I'd seen it. Then it comes to me, and I ask him with some excitement, "Did you hit that home run?" He nods exuberantly and climbs a bit further up the backstop. I tell him how great a hit it was, that it is probably still rolling down a street somewhere, and I can see not just an incredible joy on my friend's face, but an almost archetypal look, as if it were from a picture, of its being locked in, and it frames itself in my mind. My friend keeps climbing up the backstop, up under the arch that nearly goes over home plate, and he hangs there for a while like a bug. It reminds me of the lightning-bug holder that my kids use every summer, a small rounded box that has screens to give the bugs a foothold as well as air to breathe so that the children can view them inside the box after catching them. Quite typically, my kids catch so many in the hour between dusk and dark that they're crawling all over. Reluctant to let them go before bedtime, they bring the box back into the house only to find them all dead by morning as if the insects couldn't deal with captivity.

My friend continues to dangle on the backstop, crawling around, ignoring my calls for him to come down and walk back to our neighborhood. My dog needs to eat, so I say goodbye and take him home. I return later and sit on a bench near the field where I watch my friend crawling around on the field side of the backstop, wide open in every respect, but I still keep thinking of those lightning bugs. As night approaches, I see my friend has brought a flashlight, and occasionally I see him turn it on and off as he continues to crawl around. He still won't listen to me, and finally I go home.

The next morning, I go to the field, and the backstop is clear.

Someone says an ambulance had just been there, and while paramedics were prying a lifeless husk loose from the backstop, something very large with wings emerged and flew away.

Carnival Ride

I'm at a carnival where all the focus and attention is on the giant Ferris wheel, no surprise with all its lights and the stories of the great views when you get to the top. I'm with a rather large, diverse group of people, all waiting in line for what I think will just be to get a better look at it in the distance as it seems so far away. Our guide is telling us the story of the wheel, how each chair or platform held on the wheel is actually a specific age in history, picked up as it passed along through time and its revolutions, and with its particular bench or slants, perfectly suited for the curve and ultimately the repeating cycles of history.

I've heard that term used before, in school and such, but somehow I always felt that we were outside of that, above it, if you will, that we had heard this adage, "Learn the lessons of history or be doomed to repeat them," so many times that it was a kind of mantra that rendered us immune. But the guide says that is one of the lessons of history that must be learned, that nobody is immune.

Then he begins to recount history by taking each gondola in its turn, and he explains the rise and fall, the slant that took it up and brought it down, making it a fitting piece in the historical loop, perfect for locking into the hole, which is always whole at any given time, but always swallowing up new swaths of history into its mouth whenever it sees that mankind is going that familiar circular route. He emphasizes the story of the Roman Empire, which, despite how long it endured, is still just one gondola among many going in circles before us. He explains how the seeds of decadence were planted in it long before, perhaps even during its inception, much as an insect forms as a worm inside the acorn and emerges by cutting its way out, killing the acorn, but surviving on its own.

"This is the spirit of man," he declares. But I counter with a question whether it is exactly spirit itself that transcends history, at least some universal form of spirit, that some possess who are therefore above history. He answers, "More like left out of history. What a ridiculous assertion!"

And that he asks if we are all ready for the ride. Everyone nods yes in excitement. I am confused. What ride?

And then I realize that the whole ground on which we stand is being swept up at the fault line and is about to be put on its own gondola, that we are about to be added to the Ferris wheel of history, and the guide asks me, "Well, are you on board?"

When I decline, everyone else is swept up, and I am taken to the only ride available, a roller coaster with a single car in which I ride a horror filled up-and-down race to a cliff where the car goes over, and I plunge into the sea.

Fruit Garden

In my living room, there is a very unique and wonderful garden, if I can call it that. I frequently have dinner parties, and when we retire to the living room for a bit of relaxation and conversation, everyone delights in picking fruit from this garden which grows on one of the walls. Actually, it is rather more like an outpouring of vines laden with fresh fruit of various kinds. Everyone loves it and calls it one of the most remarkable things they have ever seen. Some even say it's one of the undiscovered wonders of the world.

Actually, they don't know how close they are to the truth, "undiscovered" being the key word here, for behind this cascade of thick leafy vines full of fresh fruit stands my most precious possession, a bookcase full of all the great classics of world literature, every one of them long since banned for the general position they hold in influencing the spirit of the individual to be whole. I was raised before the ban and drank deeply from the waters of the pages of these books, waters which now nourish these vines and produce this fruit, so indeed it is a kind of wonder, a miracle not only in surviving but in masking itself, continuing to do its good work through the fruit, though personally I still feel the books themselves are the real source and treasure. But I'm delighted to entertain and share the fruit with all of my guests, who are all eager to come again once they have tasted of it.

One night, a guest arrives who has never been here before. I would call him a guest of a guest. He is very curious about the vines, and when invited to try some fruit, after tasting it, he reaches between the vines, and his arm disappears in the process. He feels around and finally comes out with a book in his hand. Everyone gasps. It turns out that he is connected with the government. Soon a team arrives and dismantles the garden, cutting through the thick branches until finally reaching the bookcase through a jungle of leaves.

They take away every last tome, and I am also arrested and interrogated, but it is determined that because the vines are so thick and old, even I must have been unaware of the presence of the old collection, and so I am released with a warning to keep the story to myself because it might cause people to wonder about the contents of the books, and wondering can be a dangerous game to play.

On the way home from the police, I am stopped by one of my friends, a frequent guest to my home, who says he heard that my garden died in a blast, and how sorry he is for me, and for himself that he will never again taste of those delights again. "Never say never," I reply, reaching in my inside jacket pocket and producing a ripe, delicious pear.

My friend grabs it willingly and thanks me. Again as I walk, I pass another friend who offers similar condolences to me, and again I reach in my pocket for another pear. Soon there is a line of people in front of me, and I'm handing out fruit to them. The police see this and give chase, but they cannot keep up with me, and I continue on the run with plenty of food for thought.

Seeds

I am in school half listening to a teacher who is trying to cram something else down my throat, another concept or idea that will wake me up somehow to being a fulfilled, whole individual. Something about the story she is telling me begins to take hold somehow. I find myself not just interested but enrapt. After class when I tell her I found it more than interesting, she mentions that she could see that in my eyes and that it was like a seed had finally sprouted inside me; one that had fallen there among the many being sown. In time, I begin to feel this new life inside me, and I keep in mind that my teacher told me I must nurture it for it to grow into a tree. She says there are many people through history who are like trees, and many seeds to choose from. But one never knows how or when it will happen or if it will ever happen; or if one does start to grow whether it will eventually produce seeds like the others.

But I feel a special determination to keep this thing in me healthy, to give it every chance to thrive. At first I fear I have little room inside, that like inside a small terrarium, the sapling will quickly run out of room and be stunted in the confines.

But what actually happens is that the more this tree grows, the more sky I suddenly have, the greater expanses I feel inside me. The branches become nesting and resting areas for other ideas that might otherwise have just flown by; and I feel over time that I am growing roots into firm soil, and not only is the ground good and holding me up, but my roots are holding me in the ground, keeping it together and strong.

Over time, I finally feel that seeds are emerging, but I do not want them out in the world just yet. I tell myself that even though it might feel right to let them fly out in all directions, that there might be an adverse reaction. People might decide they are immature seeds and judge them harshly. They may make fun of me. I decide to hold each batch in its entirety year after year rather than share them; for how can I be totally sure that these seeds will do for anyone else what that one seed once did for me.

One day many years later I see my old teacher in a store and tell her how this tree has grown in me. She wonders why she has never heard about it. I explain that I was not ready, so I held onto the seeds. She frowns and explains that the world needs new seeds, that whether or not some don't like them, there is too much wasteland, too much being torn down, which must be balanced by new growth. The point is to get them out there and eventually they will have their impact one way or another, one of which is to ensure that trees and seeds everywhere are allowed to thrive.

And she warns me that I should have done it years ago because it might have helped, and that I should be careful. I'm not sure what she means, but inspired again by the woman who originally inspired and changed my life, I go home and get all the seeds and release them in one huge deluge over the city. A few weeks later, a team from a government agency comes to my home and says they have come to remove an annoying tree on their property. "What tree are you talking about?" I ask them. "There is no tree in my yard."

"The one inside you," they answer, and they take me away.

Gremlins

I seem to keep losing things, and searching for them is a very stressful sequence of an emotional pot on the stove that starts calm and ends up wildly boiling and spattering all over the place. My wife hates me when I even begin to hunt for something I can't find, but my question is always, "Why the heck can't I find it, it was here a minute ago?" No matter how hard I look, and I really scour the house, nothing turns up, except maybe something I'd given up on looking for a few days earlier on a failed search.

The problem is they all fail, and somehow always succeed, but I never find what I'm after that day. Personally, when I'm at my most insane and livid state, I really do secretly blame my wife. I gave up openly accusing her because of the problems it caused me and reprisals of the subtle kind only a person married for at least 20 years can relate to, but how can a toothbrush on the sink just disappear, or a pair of reading glasses I had one minute before seem to have taken a plunge off the face of the earth?

Now I just say that it must be those gremlins again, which is what she used to suggest when I started to blame her. Of course I say it in jest, in abject surrender to the ridiculous insanity of the things suddenly disappearing, but I detect a look in her that suggests otherwise. So rather than let it go, I nap during the day and lay awake in bed all night waiting for something, anything, with basically no real idea why I'm doing it, when all of a sudden she very quietly gets up and leaves the bedroom.

I furtively follow and at a distance see her handing my watch to an ugly creature in the living room, and I hear her tell the monster to hide it good this time.

Scientific Methods

I am a reporter covering an important story regarding leading world scientists gathering at a symposium that is set to end with a news conference in which they will formally announce that they have ruled out the possibility of God. I am hopeful to take part in the discussion because I have some questions that I believe should be considered before they issue a formal declaration. But what I encounter is a set of large doors blocked not only to the public but to all the news services. I express my concern that the scientists are seemingly gathering to make an announcement of a decision without a proper inquiry, and the symposium organizer simply takes my name and other pertinent information.

Considering there will be a news conference and that I want to be prepared, I get a pen and paper and write down my questions. Basically, what I want to ask first is how the scientists got past the Kantian refutation of all arguments for or against the existence of God as being beyond the scope of knowledge of man. Another question pertains to whatever science has said about whatever preconditions existed where the Big Bang could have happened; namely, how did that come into existence, and if it can be explained, then how did whatever brought it into existence come to exist. The idea is to take everything to a state of absolute nothingness out of which no single thing could ever come, or to explain in a simple and clear manner how something could come from nothing so that it all makes sense.

One of my colleagues tells me that these are the brightest men in the world and that they understand physics and matter, like they can see into molecules, but I answer that they don't cover the other half of existence, which pertains to spirit and intuition, and there are any number of equally brilliant advocates and apologists for this other side that science doesn't even consider because it isn't something that can be seen or measured though many would argue that it can surely be known. He wishes me good luck with that, and we go to the news conference to see what the scientists have to say.

As expected, they read a simple declaration that there is proof that rules out the possibility of God, but they do not offer it because they say it is too complicated for ordinary minds and must be initiated as part of the grand scientific scheme, and it would be, once it is completely understood and apprehended, and they add that it is available for all to spend a lifetime learning. As a result of my approaching earlier asking to speak to the scientists personally with my list of questions, and before I can ask any of them, I am arrested for sedition and dangerous thinking.

A Terminal Case

My brother has betrayed me in ways I cannot even begin to explain or comprehend, and my children are at a loss to understand why I have broken relations with this funny uncle who has always treated them so well. My explanations of the problem have always been simple, but their solution is that I forget about the whole thing like it never happened, which I find unacceptable. On occasion, when I try to address one of my brother's betrayals, my family increases their pressure on me to do what they see as the right thing. At the same time, they begin to see me as the bad guy in the whole picture.

The last thing I want to do is establish any kind of precedent or example of sibling rivalry, any hint of conflict that would give them any reason later in life to exaggerate a simple misunderstanding into a serious and permanent feud. But in another sense I have no choice under the circumstances because of what he did to me except to not speak to him unless he were to confess and apologize to me for the transgressions.

My wife goes to the pastor of our church and asks that he speak to me, and though I completely understand the religious position of turning the other cheek, forgiveness, loving one's enemy, blessing those that curse you, and all of those fine precepts, I am finding it difficult because I am the one who is cursing my brother. I have become his enemy, so perhaps I am the one who needs to be blessed and loved by him and not the other way around.

The pastor leaves me with the thought that such attitudes betray a greater love of the world than of the truth, and I leave him with the thought that when somebody totally screws you, even if it is your brother, no, especially when it is your brother, you're no longer of the world in a sense because a part of you has been killed. Yes, you have died inside.

And I realize that a part of me is indeed dead, that part of my soul is already gone, sucking the rest of it away. Then a thought strikes me that there has been too much killing myself for the people who don't care about me, and not enough living for the people who do, and the way to fix that isn't by bringing those people back into my life where they can do more harm, but to forget about them completely and focus on my wife and children. So I go to the memory bank agency to have those memories erased, but they find my issues with my brother have so completely taken over my mind and with such malignancy, that I am not a candidate for the procedure.

Angel Visitation

A spirit claiming to be an angel visits me on a supposed mission of mercy to salvage my soul, but I detect something familiar about the manner and demeanor of the spirit. To test my theory, I begin to make some rather pointed statements about my soul being unsalvageable due to injuries brought on by my demon of a mother while she was alive, and I notice that my saying these things has the effect of noticeably agitating the specter.

What I figure is that an angel would be objective and know what truth there is in anything I say, but this "angel" starts to show anger and defends my mother, not in a direct way or in so many words, but by blasting me as having brought it on myself for having been a selfish son, the same kind of statements and emotion that characterized my mother, so finally, I call her out. Still in denial, the spirit just declares that I am useless and a lost cause, and then leaves, simply disappearing, but I see a small card spinning down through the air where the spirit had stood.

When I pick up the card and examine it, I see that it's filled with personal information about me, mostly things I don't want to know like my IQ and date of death, which once you know them, fill the mind with the kind of relentless itch. The IQ thing I could live with, as the number is not too low, really only not ridiculously high, but I always argue that such things really only can be measured for a whole life, or how can anyone ascertain the IQ of Lincoln or Jefferson?

The same technique should be applied to adults, not to children. It strikes me that this card may actually be a reflection of that technique of my whole life, at which point it would be a disappointing number. But it may also be deceptive, from the devil, that the card was dropped deliberately with lies on it, for I have no doubt that the spirit of my mother did not come to visit with good intentions.

As for the death date, that is a real bugaboo because if it's correct, then I don't have much time, and it might indicate the visit was sincere and related to truly wanting to salvage my soul. In that case, I wouldn't really be able to hold the emotional part against my mother because she hasn't been an angel for very long, and this treatment of her by testing and pushing buttons was very typical of me, and driving her away upset was one of my greatest talents.

Psychic Reading

Usually I take the bus, but today it's raining, so as usual for the weather I am under a platform in the city waiting for a train to take me home after work when a lady brushes against me in the crowd, then stops and informs me that she is a psychic and has just experienced an inadvertent but powerful insight into my life through our contact. I ask if it's about my future, and she says no, that she doesn't do future per se and that it's actually about my past. I don't really understand as I thought psychics were supposed to reveal the future, but she explains that actually a psychic merely responds to whatever they see, and it could pertain to just about anything, including what's on my mind or what I've been doing, who my love interest might be, or something that happened in my childhood, that sort of thing, and she says that memory is a big part of it for some reason, and any of it could have a bearing on my future, but the future, at least as far as her gift goes, is unclear.

So I ask her what insight she had or information she received on bumping into me, and she says that twenty-five years earlier or thereabouts, I missed a bus, and it totally changed my life. But she adds that I couldn't possibly have any idea that missing the bus had any impact, but if I had gotten on that bus, my life would have been totally different. I say that at any time, any decision we make, or getting up late, can have an impact that can be huge and unforeseen, and she contradicts me and says that my missing the bus was totally different and the impact was gigantic. So I say that I suppose there must have been a girl on the bus, and we'd have met, gotten married, had kids, that sort of thing; and the psychic says it has so much greater significance than even that.

But at just that point, my train arrives. I defer to the psychic to board first where we can continue our conversation, but she says this is the "A" train, and she's waiting for the "B" train, so I decide to wait for her train as I can just get off at a "B" stop and walk a few blocks to my intended destination. As I make this decision and my train leaves, I laugh and ask her if it's a big deal, then hold out my hand for her to touch for any intuitions on what turn my life might just have taken by missing my train.

But this insults her, and she no longer wishes to speak with me. I do all I can in the next few minutes to apologize and appease her, but she is done with me. I persist in my entreaties a few minutes to no avail, and then her train arrives. I board with her, and she turns to me and says, "You probably should not have taken this train."

To this, I reply, "I thought you did not do futures."

At that moment, a man walks up and greets her with a kiss. She whispers something to him, and I don't have to be a psychic to realize that this is her husband, and everything he does to me flashes through my mind before he actually does it, which is little consolation because my future was obvious from the look in his eyes. When the train stops and they depart, the psychic looks at me on the floor and says, "It would have been better for you if you had taken the bus."

Coming Together

I have reached a strange convergence where at the same time as I appear to be falling apart physically, there is an opposite event happening in my mind as the various parts or ideas are combining me more into a whole, and what is more, it feels that this whole is greater than the sum of its parts. So while my hair and teeth are falling out, and though I am turning gray, and though my back is out, and various joints are failing, my mind is not just reaching its prime but has become in its collective awareness a kind of new embodiment that in some ways has no need of legs or arms and sees the body more as an impediment than a benefit, even though I recognize that when the body goes my mind goes with it.

The process makes me wonder whether there is some kind of meeting place along the experience of life where such a thing is the natural fruition of the human being, where just as a plant finally gives seeds just before it dies, that we start off in a very healthy form physically with an unformed spirit, and that while the body matures and eventually falls apart, the mind that was always in pieces slowly comes together in such a way that a whole new sense of spirit, a profoundly new state of mind, exists in the final stage of the disintegration of the body.

I go to see my doctor to explain to him what I feel. He tells me that this is not his expertise, but I should see a therapist, but the therapist tells me this is a natural feeling and to pursue it, but to take care of myself, focus on the body as it were, and try not to fall apart.

Though neither suggested, I go to see a man of God, a guru, and a Zen master, and all of them say they can relate to it, but none of them is old, nor is any of them falling apart physically. I believe this is something that only I can understand, though it is not something I can explain. Later though, when I am unable to care for myself and am committed to an institution, I meet other beings on a higher plane, but none of them are gods like me.

Enemies

I am seated at a round table strapped in my chair, and as I look around, every other person at the table is also strapped in. At the center of the table is a simple looking box with only a red button. All of the people at the table are struggling to get out of their bonds to be the first to push the button. In doing so, each believes that he will destroy not just all the others, but the countries they are from, so each and every one at the table has many enemies, but I can see that some are friends or have made alliances.

It appears, for example, that one is using his toes to try to help another undo a belt that ties him to his chair. It is easy enough to kick off shoes, and I wonder if whoever put us in these chairs in the first place has considered that. It occurs to me that someone might just try to flip his shoe out on the button and activate it at a distance, but apparently I know that the button will only respond to a human finger, although now having thought of this idea, suddenly shoes of all kinds start flying across the table, aimed at the button. It makes me wonder if others can read my mind. If so, they should know that I believe love and peace are the answers. But why is the mind empty of these thoughts?

I look across the table to test a theory and think to myself looking at this man, "You are incredibly stupid," at which he starts yelling at me in a language I do not understand, and perhaps he is only saying, "Stop staring at me, you idiot," so I can't draw any conclusions.

The only thing I know for sure is that I have no alliances with any of them myself, and looking at them one by one, it is obvious to me that they represent everything bad in the world from my point of view, and if somehow I can manage to undo my bonds and get to the button, I can quickly and quite easily make the world a better place. Like the others, I start struggling with my bonds but make no progress. At this point my parents come into the room and untie me, congratulating me on finally joining the real world.

Sinking Ship

I'm on a sinking ship, and every time I try to plug a hole, a torpedo fires through the hole and hits a ship of someone I know and puts a hole into it. And when they try to fix that hole or any other hole in their ship, a torpedo fires and hits a ship of someone they know, putting a hole in it that will generate a torpedo when they try to fix the hole. There are only a few degrees of separation between any of us on the sea, and the implications of one of my shots can be profound in people eventually lost and sunk as a result.

And so the ocean is literally cluttered with billions of ships, each one of them sinking and firing on other ships. Everyone is trying to keep their ship from sinking, and everyone is doing something to sink other ships, some accidental, some deliberate.

When I do finally manage to fix all the holes in my ship, even though a torpedo fires from each one, I sometimes find I have some peaceful time to relax and look out at the sea. There I can see ships going down, completely disappearing from sight. One too many holes will do that. It seems the older I get, the harder it is to keep my ship afloat. I've been hit so many times and repaired so many holes that I'm really becoming tired of the whole thing, tired of trying to get a little rest and looking out to see ships sinking everywhere, torpedo trails going this way and that, explosions far off and too close for comfort. It's just tiring to the extreme, and yet there's no way out of it.

If only there were land somewhere, some kind of ground on which everyone could stand, I'm sure we could all live in peace and harmony because if anything is clear, it's that everyone is sick of all this shooting and patching and sinking. Yes, it would be great to have some common ground on which we could stand. What a different world it would be! I'm sure everyone in every ship would agree that such a place would be wonderful, almost be like heaven compared to what we have now.

Carried by Emotions

I am in the city with my girlfriend just after a major-league baseball game. We are going home with the crowd, thousands of people all pouring out the gates going in various directions filling the sidewalks and streets. We have difficulty passing the buses as so many people are lining up to get on one or another. We are going to the elevated train to take it home, and when we reach the stairs, there's already a crowd in front of us going upstairs to the turnstile that only lets people through one at a time after each person pays the fare for the train.

As we inch forward, some young teenage boys behind us are acting very rowdy. They are not really causing trouble, but they are unruly and annoying. My girlfriend keeps whispering to me that she wishes someone would do something about them. As I look around, I can see there are actually many small groups of teenagers all acting the same way, just having fun as teenagers do.

I suggest she try to ignore them, and we continue to move forward slowly. The trains are running more often due to the time of day and the fact that there was a game. It is rush hour and a very hot day, and when we reach the stairs there is shade, and it feels good to be out of the sun. My girlfriend keeps complaining about the boys behind us as we go upstairs to the ticket agent. I pay for both of us and go through the turnstile first to the open air platform and wait for her. When I look back, she has stopped just after going through the turnstile and will not let anyone through.

She motions for me to come over and help, so I go over to her just as the crowd behind starts yelling for her to move. As she advances, she keeps pressing herself back against the boys who are now, it seems, putting their hands on her. She looks at me and throws up her arms as if to say "Why don't you do something about this?" Rather than get involved, I stand and wait for her to cut herself loose and watch as she and the boys become a wall and a roof, while I become a strut that holds up the other side of the roof as it forms over to me.

All of us are now part of the station. People pass by us night and day and take umbrage beneath us from the elements. The boys continue to hold her and anger her on their end, while on mine her bolts are forever ready to pop. Over time even the green paint, globbed on thick by city workers, does not soften her hard look in the slightest as she glares through all the layers like some demon in a ceiling fresco.

Siren Song

I am Odysseus, King of Ithaca trying to make my way back home and I've been informed that I'm about to pass through a particularly dangerous area where the sirens will sing and anyone who overhears them will jump off ship and swim to their total destruction. I'm intrigued by this and want to hear the song so I have instructed the men to tie me to the mast and put wax in their ears.

As we enter the region of the sirens, my men are working on deck. I had told them to ignore the island, not even to look its way, and go about their work. Meanwhile I hear something in the distance and lose consciousness. When I wake I am suddenly filled with a sense that I'm on a mission. The mission was to get to this island. I need to get there. But my men have apparently mutinied and tied me to the mast.

The women on the shore I can see are saying something to me but I can't seem to hear it. For some reason it is like wax is growing in my ears. I hear it less and less and yet I know I must listen. I am striving so hard to hear I crane my neck and cry to my men to untie me, that I need to hear their singing. I tell them to quiet down, that the noises they're making are blocking the sirens' voices, and I need to hear their song.

The whole reason I have sailed to this island is to hear what they are saying but somehow I don't know what has happened. Something must have intervened, making me a prisoner on my own ship, and now I have a problem with my ears. Wax is growing in them so thick now that I have failed entirely to hear anything they have said to me. It appears the rest of the crew have the same problem because they can't hear me, so the mission is a failure. As the sirens disappear from sight, exhausted from struggling, I collapse and lose consciousness.

When I wake up, I see my men have untied me. They want to know what I heard. They ask me to please tell them about the song of the sirens and what it sounded like. I tell them the truth, which is that I do not know. For some reason I did not hear them. It all just went by like there was nothing. I do not know what it was like, only that I missed the entire thing but would gladly have given my life to get closer to hear anything, even a whisper, from my beloved sirens.

Life in a Nutshell

While reading the newspaper I see there is a contest with a large monetary prize for anyone who can put the meaning of life in a nutshell. The very fact the rules are stated as such is amazing to me because some years earlier I had done just that. I put the meaning of life very neatly and carefully in a nutshell. It took a lot of time and effort, and I could write a book on the difficulty of making it all fit in such a tiny space. But I achieved it, and now if I can only find it, it looks like I'll be rich because I know my entry would win this contest easily.

So I start looking all around my office for the nutshell. I really have accumulated a lot of stuff though. I routinely straighten up a little here and there, but obviously over the 20 years I've been using this space since I made the nutshell, it's gotten a little away for me. There's lots of books, computer equipment, paintings, shelves completely overloaded with stuff, file cabinets full of stuff, boxes, milk crates, full drawers, crammed closets; so much stuff it looks like I'll never find such a little thing in all this mess, not by the contest deadline anyway.

My wife suggests I just go ahead and duplicate it, start over and put the meaning of life in a nutshell again. To me, that is just one crazy idea. After all I did the first time to get it right, I know I would just be way off the mark trying to remember what I did and how I did it, when what it takes to do it in the first place is a wholehearted and sincere grasp and focus on the meaning of life, not some secondhand longing for a repeat performance.

So I step outside my house and try to think by looking at it where I might have tucked away that precious little long-forgotten perfect nutshell. In my mind, I go from room to room, each having its own pile of junk, its own network and maze of drawers crammed with junk. The walk-in closet in the basement is so overloaded just with memorabilia it would take a week to go through it. I can't even use the garage for a car because it's so packed with boxes. I realize it's just futile to even begin the search, and so I go back to my regularly scheduled tedium resigned to the fact that I'll never find it.

As the contest deadline passes, even though I know I'll never be rich, what is more important is that the meaning of life is not lost. I know it's neatly tucked away in a perfect little nutshell, somewhere close under all this junk.

The Ascent

I am in the base camp of a great mountain where people come from all over the world to try to get to the summit. Personally, I'm more than happy to just sit and gaze at the mountain, it's so inspiring. My spirit soars when I think of going up there, standing at the top with a flag and coming back with a picture to prove I made the climb. But my life is basically driven in support of the supreme effort. There's a lot that needs to be done here in the foothills, and one might say that I fight in the front lines, and the metaphor is valid because much of the time, it really is a battle.

There are all kinds of things I have to put up with, drunks who brag about their previous exploits, then chicken out of any attempt at the ascent. Fights are always breaking out, and I have found myself in the middle of them, and on the floor, trying to break them up. I've gotten used to this life now that I think about it, and I can't imagine anything else.

Often people have an extra place for an experienced climber and invite me to go along, but I always refuse. The few times I've actually tried to make the ascent, I honestly didn't like the feeling of the rarefied atmosphere, and although I like the view, it was spoiled by the bodies of climbers who did not make it before, who were left behind as it's too difficult to bring them down.

In a sense, the fight to get to the top is like a visit to a cemetery. One hears the stories of failure in the same sentence as a success, and though they say there is always room at the top, it isn't like there isn't a huge risk or price to pay. So the top has a kind of built-in bottom, and I have found that aspect highly unpleasant.

The bottom where I work is more of a moderate experience. I'd call it more middle-of-the-road. It's safe, and even an avalanche will die out before it reaches the camp. I still dream of going, of making the climb, of standing at the top. That dream has been in me since I was a boy. But now I just see the journey to the peak as a road with a steep incline calling people to take the serious chance to see what they're made of.

So while they try to live that dream, I hand out drinks and warm blankets, wish them good luck and cheer them on. I rise and fall with their success and failure, but though I know I'm performing a great and necessary service, inside I cry that our roles are not reversed, and at night as I try to sleep, I imagine myself climbing and making it, every time. I've been there a thousand times in my mind, but during the day, I work hard and never ask why they cannot wash my dishes and let me hold their flag.

Big Plans

I have a wonderful idea and feel the need to express it visually, so I begin a search for materials that leads me to a barrel of nine sticks that look like they will serve as I wish to lay something out over a wide area. But strange as it may sound, these sticks turn out to be some kind of industrial waste and are magnetic, so as I pull them apart and lay them out, they keep rolling back toward one another and snapping together, and I cannot use them to do the job.

In my next attempt, I cut nine limbs from a tree and size them according to the idea I have, and when I am finished, I have a barrel of sticks similar to those that were magnetic.

But when I begin to lay them out, even a slight puff of wind is all it takes to blow them out of place, for they lack the weight of the ones that were magnetic.

Then I think that perhaps I can start digging and make the rendering as an impression of the earth, but the grass is too thick, and on such an angle that I cannot see anything I have done. So I get a sheet of paper and do a drawing, and while I am somewhat happy with the results, what I really wish for is an outdoor piece, and installation, that will be there like the Great Wall of China or like Pompeii, where even after thousands of years, if even a part of it is discovered, the rest will be excavated and restored in order that future generations will be able to marvel as well.

What I would really like to do is somehow preserve an area of the desert under a dome and make my nine marks in the sand. The dome will protect the work from the wind, and people will be allowed to come near it without disturbing it. I am thinking a thousand square miles will do because I would like it to be visible from space. Though I realize the idea has evolved considerably from my original intentions, it is worth it. Even now it is growing even more amazing, including all the planets, but still more difficult to accomplish unless Pluto regains its planetary status so I can include it as one of them.

The Critic

I am attending, hosting and appearing as the star attraction of what amounts to my coming-out party, and even if it is unusual in the sense that such events are usually held for young people and I am weighed down with age and infirmity, all appears to be going fairly well. When young people ask why I waited so long, I just tell them the truth, which is that I wanted to wait until I finished the main works, got everything not just done but right as it were, and as we look around the room, it does appear to have been worth waiting for.

But as always with such "openings," there is a critic somewhere who seems to delight in picking everything apart and declaring it substandard. There's one here as well, evidently. Some of my friends point him out to me, and I see him walking around with his hands behind his back, glaring at my various phases and accomplishments.

As he seems to ponder them, he also appears disinterested, more absorbed in the bowls of snacks placed at various stations around the room. While nibbling on these and lost in thought, he notices we are looking his way and approaches us. He immediately goes into a kind of diatribe on the whole affair, comparing my efforts to a variety of other works out there, declaring mine don't pass muster but that the snacks are very tasty and tastefully displayed.

I have always despised this type of person and see critics as parasites, and so I ask, "What gives you the authority to measure anything? Is there an ammunition dump where you load up after a simple education of the status quo, after which you shoot down anything that's new unless it moves not in deference to the monuments to the dead, but according to your idea of what's fashionable?"

My organizers are doing face palms as to them my words are a breach of ethics and ruinous to me, like a fire is already sweeping through the place, destroying everything. My critic just stares at me. I am determined and just stare back, so focused that I don't see anything else around me. The room fades out. All my works are gone. It's just him and me, and we do this for the longest time until I realize the room isn't there either. I am just sitting in a chair in my basement office. And in the back of my mind I can hear my critic say, "All you ever had to do was ignore me, but you're too much of an idiot to even do that. That's why you'll never succeed or have a show or coming-out party." He's right. I am my own worst critic and enemy.

Voters

I'm at a village meeting where a vote is on the floor to finally and permanently remove all dialogue and wording from daily minutes regarding the other side of the mountain. This terminology has always had a place in my life. Since I was a boy, my father used to talk about how he dreamed, and how his father used to dream of moving there. I heard all about my father's plans every night at the dinner table while I was growing up, like the other voters at the meeting, I guess it's fair to say that I am more than a little sick of the other side of the mountain. All the kids in my generation used to fight over who would have the biggest house when we all moved there, and yet here we are, all still locked in our marriages, mortgages, and jobs, not one of us ever having made the journey.

But to remove the language of the other side of the mountain strikes me as extreme since that dream has always been part of our heritage. Yes, I understand that it inculcates a reasonable expectation that is surely followed by an ultimate disappointment, but I don't think it's the business of the assembly to dictate what I should tell my own children, whether I should not relate such dreams to them and not be able to pass on the whole other side of the mountain mentality.

Another thing that bothers me is the motion on the floor to remove any voter from the assembly who votes against the motion to eliminate the wording. I worry that all votes will be monitored and that merely to vote that a person should not be eliminated for not going along will get me eliminated. It is intimidating, and I put forward a motion that the discussion be tabled at least for one day so that we might all go home and think about what we're doing.

Surprisingly, my motion carries, but the leadership makes a stern speech with plenty of threats and warnings of what is important as our duty to perform when we reconvene. When I get home, my wife notices my awful mood, and I tell her I think it's time we consider pulling up stakes and finally pioneering our way out of this lousy valley for the sake of our kids.

I appeal to the portraits of our fathers and grandfathers on the wall, to their dreams of a better life, and I recommend that we depart under the cover of darkness. She agrees, and we pack our things and set out with sleepy kids to the mountain pass we have never actually seen. Surprisingly, we find the way crowded with other vehicles all headed in the same direction.

Master of the House

I am at the dinner table with my family, surveying how it has grown in my fifty years as lord and master of the house, and between all my wives and children, grandchildren and great-grandchildren, there are so many people they don't even hear me as I stand up to make a proclamation of thanks for the meal we are about to receive.

I am not even sure of the total number, but I stopped counting at more than a hundred wives. Most of the children they had are here with their wives, husbands and children, and some of those children have families, so I can only guess that there are more than a thousand people here today.

Only a few seats away sits my first-born son talking to his brother, and though they sit close to me, it's so loud in here I can't hear what they're saying, but I can guess they're having one of their typical disagreements about politics. I always stressed a specific line of thought in raising my children, but I was frankly always amazed at how they diverged from my thinking, and one another's, to the point that I have little doubt that for the most part everyone in this room has a different point of view even though we are all one and of the same genetic information, linked by marriage and birth.

I know I am only one man, but given my stature, I can say proudly that beyond this hall where my family dines tonight, lies my kingdom, and a fine people it is over whom I rule. Again, I extend a single line of thought, but I have no doubt that each person has a singular and differing point of view. But at least they recognize my authority and quiet down when I'm about to speak, though I am told that only those people in attendance at my speeches are listening, and that the shops are full and active elsewhere.

I chalk this up to the fact that life goes on everywhere even though there may be a focus in the center. Again I stand up to say something but again my family ignores me. It is interesting to me that this group I have played a big part in assembling, that in many ways wouldn't be here without me, hardly notices I am here and certainly will not miss me when I am gone. But I have this excellent gold watch they presented to me last year, and I've been watching people stare at it all through the night.

The Conveyor

I am riding the conveyor of my life, a kind of carrier that I really never felt was moving, until it suddenly stops and lets me out onto a platform with basically everything I own, a process that takes a while because I have a lot of stuff. When that's done, I stand there wondering what's next, and I see another conveyor nearby that I instinctively know is the one I'm supposed to take going forward if I want to properly unwind all of my positions. Taking a ride on this thing, I think to myself, is not like going forward. The idea is that by the time I reach the end of the line, all my stuff will be gone, properly disposed of, sold and converted into cash, making it easy for my heirs as they won't have to sift through a lot of junk.

It's somewhat unattractive as an option in many ways, and I have thought about this a lot, but I've frankly never been ready to admit that the time had come for me to start this process. For me, part of the affirmation of life is to keep living it and enjoying it, not looking at it as having a finish with loose ends to tie up. That's just depressing, so basically I've put it all off, the selling and dissemination of my possessions, and just continued the process of collecting like there's no end in sight.

All I have to do is push a button for the process to transfer to the other conveyor to begin, but I hesitate. Don't I have any other options, I wonder? It just seems wrong that I should need to start going downhill all of a sudden. In another way, I feel the purpose of the conveyor of life is to show me what I have, which is clear to me as I stand before the pile, but why does it follow that I need to unwind my positions and get out of everything? So I look around the platform for any other option, and I find a rusted door blocked with boards and marked "Keep Out" with yellow tape.

I remove the boards and tape and push my way through and see it's another conveyor, obviously not used in a while, but it seems that it would allow me to continue my life. So I push a button, and it collects all my things, and I'm back the way I was before, only now I can feel I'm moving. I feel every bump and heave. Boxes fall and become worthless to me. There's a fire that rages through half my stuff before I can put it out. A hole opens in the ceiling through which water pours and ruins much of what I have left.

Then, short of the arrival point by many years, there's a terrible malfunction that mangles me in the machinery, destroying the rest of my stuff as well. Afterwards, they sweep me out with the garbage, and block the door and tape it shut for the next guy.

Trailblazer

I am a trailblazer, or at least that is what I always wanted to be, and what I always tried to be when I was a kid. There really weren't that many trails to blaze, I know, the world having been pretty much totally discovered by then, but I never tired of reading books about such heroes, and I loved movies on those subjects. But as for true trailblazing, cutting one's own path through the wilderness, hoping not to run into dead ends, or life-threatening dangers or to run out of provisions, I know there weren't any openings for that, unless I wanted to go up to the Canadian tundra of the Northwest Territories, I suppose, where I'd probably be breaking laws, not to mention destroying delicate ecosystems that might never come back from the damage caused by my footprints. No, I had to be content with the concept of blazing a trail in whatever area or field of activity I chose as my work. One can blaze trails in science and medicine, for example, find new cures and therapies; and one can blaze new trails in industry, isolate and develop new sources of energy, and manufacture new machinery to simplify tasks and reduce risks to people.

There isn't a field that doesn't need trailblazers, so I knew that I could cut out my place in my work even though it meant I had my work cut out for me, or something like that.

So I chose a field in which I thought there was plenty of jungle left so to speak, huge intellectual forests and wastelands on a metaphorical plane, which was basically in metaphysics, particularly in the humanities. Without going into great detail of the exact nature of my work, suffice it to say that when I started, it was like bailing out of a plane over Burma and just landing out in the middle of the jungle. Over the next forty years, to extend the metaphor, I cut through wide swaths of jungle, came down with this fever and that fever, forded this and that river, having no contact with the world in all that time.

I did not meet many other trailblazers along the way. I found the territory virgin, and using every known technique I could bring to bear through my education and experience, I found that the jungle educated me, gave me experience, made me more aware than anyone I've heard of in books of its canopies, its textures, its living, breathing state. All the while I kept detailed journals and records of my exploits, knowing that one day I would emerge and be finally able to reveal what I had accomplished and add to the history and knowledge of the jungle, and perhaps find my way to a university where I'd be seen as an expert, a mentor, a teacher and professor.

But when I came out finally emerged from the jungle, everyone was just amazed. They didn't know what I was talking about. "Jungle?" they asked me. "What jungle?" In all those years, I was so caught up in its mysteries that I hadn't realized it was all being discarded. As preferences evolved to virtual realities and the various gadgets that allowed people to navigate a crowded and complex jungle-free existence with literally millions of trails from which to choose, they decided they didn't need the jungle anymore, and trailblazers like me became obsolete.

Variations

After a somewhat reckless youth, I have decided that I must settle down. So I marry and take a job my father-in-law offers me and begin to live in a very structured environment. I adopt an attitude that the many variations of my previous life can be found in a single theme, that enjoyment can be found in repetition and structure.

So I get up every day at the same time and look out the window. One day it is sunny. Another it is raining. That is a variation. As I drive to work, one day certain lights are green, another day they are red. That is another variation. All around me there are new things every day, little differences that I can appreciate if I only look for them. A slight cool breeze today feels very different than the hot wind yesterday. The long train that stops me today is going much more slowly than the one that stopped me yesterday, and so forth.

In the office, it is the same story. The tie I am wearing today is a different color. The coffee is fresher because I arrived a few minutes earlier. There's a new secretary working for one of the associates. It is amazing what variety there is if I only think about it.

But after a while a breeze is a breeze, and a train is a train. Traffic is a pain, and the office coffee is awful. I hate wearing ties, and six months out of every year the weather is lousy. I miss my life in the fast lane and my friends at the bar. I look at the way I am thinking as a variation in my mood.

Just as I accept each new variation in the day, I accept these new variations of mood where one day I wish I were back with a former girlfriend instead of my wife because today's variation of marriage is another dose of bad cooking, a different dish, but is as badly made as the one I had trouble swallowing yesterday. Buffalo wings and a couple of pitchers of beer sound like a nice variation to my ears.

So I'm sitting in my office dreaming of the old days when I notice my watch has stopped. It's a really nice one my father-in-law gave me as a wedding present, gold with all kinds of special things like chronograph, numerical date, weekday, twenty-four-hour hand, moon phase, and other features.

I worry it's broken and set it down on my desk for a moment when I hear something calling to me. It's coming from the watch. Suddenly the whole face of the watch grows into a kind of portal leading to what appears to be a night scene. I look into the watch and can see all the way down the street, bar after bar, and man, is it ever calling to me!

So I go in, but first I take off my tie. And I stop at the first bar I see and meet new people. I stay there a while and then go home with one of the girls that I meet. I stay at her apartment until I find a place of my own. I really live it up for a long time, but I keep thinking everything is okay because my watch has stopped.

So it goes on for years and years. Finally I've had enough, and the doctor tells me my liver is damaged, and none of the people I've met who I thought were my friends really gives a damn about me, so I try to find my way out, back up the street and out of the dial of what is now a cheap watch, and I find myself in a shabby basement of a dumpy restaurant, where a fat guy in a t-shirt and apron is yelling at me that my break is over and to quit my daydreaming and get back to work doing dishes.

Drum Spirits

I'm supposed to go chop some wood in the back, but I have a number of reasons why I don't feel like doing it. First, it's hot. My wife and I live on the edge of the jungle, but being outside of it doesn't keep this place from feeling like a jungle. The hot wind blows night and day. Second, I'm not in great shape. I'm getting older, and I fear I'll hurt my back. Finally, the wood my wife wants me to chop is an old, well-polished log that we found here when we cleared away the jungle, and I've always liked it. It's really beautiful and makes a nice bench. But she catches me sitting on it and really starts yelling for me to get to work.

So I go to get the axe. When I pull it out of the box in the shed, I don't notice the metal head falling off. When I get to the log and start swinging, there's no cutting, only these beautiful tap tones ringing out. They're so nice, I pound for a while longer, not knowing that this is an old tribal log drum, and my pounding has sent out an inexplicable, undecipherable message in a jumbled order, and it has awakened the great spirits that normally expect a message they will be able to understand.

So the spirits convene and in failing to transcribe the message to infer its meaning, they conclude it must simply be a wake up call because that is what it did, it woke them up, similar to an alarm clock.

Meanwhile my wife has heard the pounding, and despite my declarations that we should save the log as it makes such beautiful tones, she scoffs and orders me to get the axe head back on the handle and get back to work. So I dig in the bin until I find it, then slip it back on and pound the handle on the ground to set the head firmly into the handle.

By now the spirits are wondering about the silence as they sit awaiting further orders, when all at once they cringe at the sounds of gashes being made, of a splintering and severing of the holy link between two worlds, and without even trying to decipher the code, they discern its meaning and rush to the site where they find me sweating and swinging an axe into the drum log, each cut sending pieces in different directions.

The spirits hover around doing everything they can to put an end to the terrible noise signaling the destruction of a means to contact them in a lost language. And since I am unaware of both the spirits and the language they understand, I just keep swinging until finally I cut through the thing, making it more easily transportable to the wood pile.

Once my wife and I carry the pieces and stack them, we go back, and she immediately starts making plans for the garden she will have in its place. But now I feel inklings of what I've done as the spirits have finally awakened fully and have figured out how to communicate with me. I can see and feel them now hovering about. I know they are angry and wish to make me pay for what I've done. At the same time, I know they wish to make me take the place of the log, now that they have established communications with the world through me. I wish I could say I'm sorry and explain that I don't want the job, but I have yet to learn how to communicate with them. All I can do is gesticulate wildly. My wife thinks I'm crazy, and the spirits are confused, and neither the physical nor spiritual world gives me any peace.

Dissemination

I have something I think important and significant enough to say to the entire human race, but in order to gain clearance to say it, I must submit an application to the authorities who monitor what things the human race is allowed to hear. The disseminators, as they're called, have a long list of criteria that I must meet, and the failure to meet any criterion will be enough for them to refuse me.

They first need to check my appearance, the sound of my voice, how I convey myself, do I have good charisma and camera appeal, do I make good eye contact, all those sorts of things. They may determine that I am unsuitable for television but may give me a green light for radio. The next thing they check is my history. In this they have a lot of latitude, but a lot of complex algorithms must be used to ascertain a final number. If my score comes in under this number, it's no go. If over, then I am okay. They look back all the way to early grades in elementary school, to achievement tests and IQ scores. They check middle school records, though these count least in scoring, and finally high school and further education, including college and graduate school. They also check credit history and job security, essentially seeing what one has been up to in private life. They check all background information, tax returns, police reports, anything and everything pertinent to determining whether there are any hidden agendas or character flaws.

However these stack up, they ultimately arrive at this magic number, and if you meet requirements, then they ask for a transcript of everything that you plan to say to the human race. Your words are then checked for authenticity and authority. Are you the originator of these thoughts, and are you qualified to say them? They check as well for the reading level of the thoughts you plan to deliver. Will people understand them? Are they suitable for children? Once they determine that these thoughts have not been borrowed or stolen and are indeed suitable for an audience capable of understanding them, depending on your status based on numbers derived from your age, wealth, fame, and importance in the community, you are assigned a time slot for a reading that will be monitored, prerecorded, so that you don't intentionally go off script.

They do make changes and what they give back to you is what you must read. Usually it is very close to your original, but you also want a time slot closer to prime time, so as not to be lost after midnight when everyone is sleeping. Then when you read, whatever it is you have to say, the final matrix of ideas is applied that basically crops whatever you say into a sound bite, a context, meaning out of everything you say, only a small portion is broadcast in order to cast you in a particular light. If anything you have to say goes against standards and views held by the disseminators, it is likely you will come off as a crank no matter how inspiring and compelling your speech. But if you are lucky enough to make it through the process, it is a great honor to even have a few words get to the ears of the entire human race, even at four in the morning, even if you are taken out of context and made to look bad. Ultimately it is a privilege and honor, and you should not only try to compose your thoughts according to what you think they would want you to say, but thank the disseminators for their consideration whether or not you make it through thought processing.

Western Theme

I am a cowboy, or at least I look like one, all dressed up in boots, chaps, western shirt, vest, and a ten gallon hat, just like my brother who has managed to get me so mad that I finally throw down my hat, which means at this point that the fight is to the death because it's been escalating all day long. We've both been up and squabbling since dawn, only I've been trying along the way to end the skirmishes because it all started over something very petty, a piece of candy that we couldn't split that he stuck in his mouth with a great grin. He could have chewed it up or swallowed it, but he chose to suck on it slowly, where every so often when things cooled down he would show it to me, still in his mouth, still pretty big, and laugh in my face, trying to egg me on.

Now it is getting late, and our parents are getting ready to saddle up and start the long drive home. As we're gathering our things, my hat hits me hard in the face, courtesy of my brother who found it on a chair. He now sits there, legs crossed, much as if rolling a cigarette under a hot sun, checking his pockets for matches, only he's too young to smoke and already has something in his mouth, and as I look at him, still fuming over the thrown hat, he bares his teeth and shows me he still has plenty left of the candy he's been storing in his cheeks. I still don't want to fight, but for him the declarations of war have already been signed. In a few minutes we'll be riding together in the back seat of the car, and I know he'll be biding his time, waiting for me to settle in, before punching me in the ribs, then whistling Dixie so that if I complain to my parents he'll have that look of total innocence, which always leads to my getting pistol whipped from the front seat.

Now he shifts his weight to show me that he's been sitting on my stuff, trying to get me to come over and hit him, but angry as I feel, and though I know I can't get out of this, I find myself going over everything, trying to figure out what went wrong and when we crossed over where there was no going back. I can see he's not thinking about any of that. He's glad we're going to be fighting all night. It almost seems like he's been waiting for this his whole life, like this is what he was made for, and though all he has on above his waist is a cowboy shirt, string tie, vest and black hat, it almost seems like he's a gladiator girding on chest armor and helmet. There's a kind of gleam in his eyes, something like joy except it's aimed at my neck like a lasso that will tighten as the horse rides away to pull off my head.

Some of the friends he made on this visit, the ones he turned against me, enter the room to say goodbye. They all have their cowboy clothes on as well except for one who's dressed up like an Indian who crossed over to join their evil gang and now stands with them even against his tribe. They all shake hands before looking across the room at me as if to say that they now know where I live, and that they'll soon be coming out to visit us, maybe next summer, at which point they'll be sure to look me up on boot hill or help me find a nice place there. I could also see that my brother was the central figure of this mad posse, that they were taken in by his smooth, trash-talking ways and intimidated by that quick temper of his, which would flare up the second anyone questioned anything he said like I always did.

But now he only barks at them while he always looks at me with a sly smile, showing me that piece of candy whenever he can. It's like throwing kisses to someone hog-tied and set to be dragged across the prairie by a horse as soon as it's whipped across the flank. Everything in his demeanor is coiled up like a snake ready to strike any second, watching me every second, flicking his tongue with that candy, testing the air and daring a first response.

I know I'll soon be tangled up in a rope and throwing punches at him, hoping to make him gasp for breath such that maybe he'll choke on whatever's left of the candy, but I can almost see him faking that for effect, then showing me it's all gone, and then later coming up with it again. I know I can't go to my parents, tug on a sleeve and get an ear. They act like they've seen it all too many times to be bothered by it, and they don't know how dire it has gotten. But in my mind, I still feel that there's good in me but not in him because I'm thinking about it, trying to figure it out, wishing it weren't happening, longing for a peaceful solution even when any hope of that is long gone. Sadly, it seems to be when I drift off and think this way that I'm caught off guard as if I've fallen asleep. Suddenly, I'm covered by five guys, pounding and punching me, my brother standing above, kicking me in the ribs. Obviously my parents must have left the room for a few seconds, and I don't say anything about it when they return moments later. The boys just move away laughing as if they were just having a little bit of fun. My parents only smile because they didn't see anything, and they don't notice the residual look of bloodlust in their eyes, but I can see how they enjoyed punishing me and what kind of people they are and how there's nothing I can do but fight. As I get into the back seat, my brother kicks me in the stomach and knocks the wind out of me, and it's all I can do to ask my father to turn up the song on the radio, which is "Ghost Riders in the Sky," and the trip home begins on a western theme.

Totem Pole

I am a totem pole, a stack of unhappy faces, each being not just a personality but a separate entity, and my own particular conscious state is located at the bottom, where my mother told me from the very beginning that I would always be. She was quite the totem pole herself, and of the totems in our family, she was tallest and loudest, with the grimmest and most ebullient faces on top of one another. Her own particular conscious state was at the top of her totem, so she ruled those beasts, told them when to shut up and also let them have their way when it suited her, letting them gang up on us.

I don't think I really liked any of them, but being on the bottom from my own perspective, I really didn't much like the ones on top of me, the way they played up to her, seeking her approval. I didn't like the way she rewarded them for putting me down. She would laugh, all of her faces would, when I was being ridiculed. I could not stand it, but I had to take it.

My father didn't do much about it. At the top of his totem, it was all business faces, a serious breadwinner bent on kissing all the rears of his boss's totem in order to succeed. He treated all of my faces the same, business-like, and he rarely even acknowledged me on the bottom, though once or twice he quelled a particularly brutal verbal attack or two, sparing me a few minutes of further humiliation even though I had learned to ignore it.

I was immune and numb to it all by a certain point. I knew my other faces needed me in certain situations. Without me, they really wouldn't have made it through school, I knew that, and they knew that, but did they ever thank me? No, and when the grades came home, my mother's happy faces would kiss them one by one, but never me. It was like she didn't even know I was there.

I'm not sure how I ever got through that part of my life except I think it made me stronger to go unrecognized on the bottom, and I like to think I carried the others all that time, and I loved my parents despite the way their faces were stacked. I always thought they were sad people despite the stack of smiling heads; and despite all my frowns, I had always considered myself happy in spirit.

Finally when I was of age and about to leave home, I was at the doctor who for the first time administered personality tests, and he came back with some startling results.

The testing basically indicated that I had been raised upside down and needed to be flipped, so he conducted the procedure, and suddenly I was on top, and all smiles, head to toe head. From my new perspective, my mother is none too happy with the arrangement. I realize she was all frowns and has been all along, but she has no control even over herself I can tell, and I'm just glad I finally see things now as they really are.

Support Chip

I discover I'm terminally ill, and I worry that I am leaving the world at a time when my son really needs me as he's just graduating high school, and there are so many big years ahead of him, when the doctor informs me of a new technology that I may want to consider. Basically it involves a transfer of my psyche to a computer chip that would be implanted in my son. It would have to be done soon, when I'm still in a relatively healthy state of being and mental awareness. If I wait too long, then the transfer will not be successful, or it will transfer me with a decreased mental capacity.

The process would end my physical life sooner, but it will allow me to react when my son is experiencing stress, and not just react but "reactivate" so to speak. At those moments, I would appear as a kind of fully-aware hologram and have mobility within ten feet of him. I'd be able to correspond with him, understand the situation and offer him advice. My wife passed away a few years ago, and this is my only son, so I explain it to him, and he consents to the procedure, knowing that I'll be there for him when he needs me.

The designers aren't entirely sure how long the chip will survive in him, but they believe I would survive as a projection longer than I would as a human being even if I had not gotten sick. But I would only be projected for "short bursts" as they explain it to me. So one day my son and I go to the hospital and undergo the procedure. All I remember is that they put a mask on my face and told me to relax and breathe deeply.

The next thing I know, I am standing next to my son as he is being beaten in an alley by thugs. I try swinging at one of them, and my arm goes through him like a ghost. My sudden appearance scares them away, and I speak to my son about the dangers of walking home alone at night. But as he calms down, I go unconscious again, returning to the chip. The next thing I know, I'm standing with my son in the hospital at the birth of his child, but the child is dying. I end up staying a couple of days through that one, but when his stress level drops, I disappear again. Immediately for me, I am back in what is a few years for him. His wife has died. Again, I stay a few days and try to help him. Even as I finally disappear into the chip, I'm still worried about what he is going to do as he is still in such despair.

But all of this is getting stressful for me as well since it's just constantly negative. Whenever I leave, I'm instantly back in another debacle. I don't feel how many years have gone by. To me it is all happening in immediate sequence, and I get no rest, so I find myself blowing my top at some point, at the fifth or so time in a row that I find him drunk on the street but cannot lift him up. He gets sick of seeing me, then stops listening. He seems to have learned how to shut me off and tune me out.

Finally I appear and he's dead, and for some reason, I'm stuck "on" and can't shut down. After his burial, I am still being projected by him, but I cannot stray or I will simply disappear and then reappear where I was as a new projection, so I sit on his grave like a loyal hound, waiting for the chip to finally fail.

Bird Soap

I am watching television, and I see a commercial that grabs my attention. It is for a new product called "Great Wings" for a bar soap with special agents that are absorbed through the skin as the soap is used in showering. These agents cause the user to experience a heightening of natural powers, give one the feeling of having a pair of great wings, where one acquires a sense that one is flying, no, soaring above the world, able to take everything in by just glancing around rather than slowly experiencing the world by winding one's way around slowly like a worm. At the end of the commercial, the great symbolic bird swoops down and devours the tiny worm that is helplessly squirming on the ground.

I am totally smitten with the desire to buy this product and use it on myself in the hope of undergoing this promised transformation. Though it is not cheap, I eagerly fork over the dough for a few boxes, fearing I should stock up a bit as I would have expected it to sell out quickly given what it can do. Once home, I head into the shower right away to begin the process, and as I soap it on, I immediately begin to sense a tingling in my skin, and I feel the joy of euphoria drying off, which confirms that it is already working.

When I visit my family and tell them about it, rather than pat me on the back and congratulate me, they unexpectedly frown and warn me that there may be consequences to my use of this product. I cannot believe their selfishness, and I tell them I already feel like I am better off after only one shower. Later, I go home and head to the shower again and use the bar of soap shaped like a great bird twice as much, so that when I finish, the outline and shape of the bird in the soap is less defined, the wings way more smooth.

Within a few days, I'm already on the second bar, and the results of taking five showers a day are starting to show themselves. While one might expect dry skin that would be peeling and raw, I am actually seeing signs that my skin is toughening up. But also, I am actually growing feathers. It scares me at first, but the agents in the soap bring on such confidence and euphoria that not only do I continue to use it, I buy more and shower all day long, even in cold water, and I'm in ecstasy. I feel like I'm dancing in a bird bath or a blocked gutter.

Becoming a bird I find is so much better than being human. After a week of this, I stand before a mirror and relish in how I've been transformed into a great bird. I fly over to see my family, but they are horrified. They get guns. I fly off into the sky and they give chase, taking my father's plane up to follow me. I hide in a cloud, and inside the cloud it starts to precipitate. The rain begins to wash over, dissolving me like a bar of soap into just bubbles and so much suds, all of which falls to earth like bird droppings, and by the time the cloud disappears, there is no sign of me.

Book of Life

I'm with my dying father trying to offer him comfort, but I feel I'm doing worse than he is as he seems content in his passing. He asks me to pass him a book on the shelf behind me, which isn't so much a book to read but a portfolio of pictures and personal notations. He sits up and begins to browse through it for one last time, smiling as he encounters each face in a picture, pausing to reflect on who these people were and what they each meant to him in his life. As he does so, a few things fall out of my father's book, and I stoop to pick them up for him. As I hand them to him one at a time, he carefully puts each back in its proper place, and I ask what the book is all about.

He explains that it is a record he kept, going back to his high school days, of people who mattered to him, that the book is filled with pictures of people who died along the way, starting with the war, which claimed many of his friends.

So I comment that it seems to be a kind of book of death, and he snaps back, coughing a little as he says with the energy that he has left, that, no, it is a book of life, and it contains the living memory of people he loved whose memory he has held in his heart all these years.

I meant nothing disrespectful in anything I said, so I apologize, which he happily accepts. A few days later, he dies. After this, I consider that while I have many memories of old friends, not many have died, but I don't have what could be considered as a book of life. So I buy a portfolio and begin it by thinking of old friends I haven't seen in a while and looking them up on the computer, then writing in their current address and phone numbers. I then put the book on the shelf, but one day I feel like perhaps I should reach out to these people with whom I haven't spoken in many years, and so I pick up the phone and start dialing.

What's sad is I find that these people I pulled up in thought as being important to me have very little recollection of me and have no time to sit and reminisce. I am very disappointed that they didn't really hold onto any memories of me, but I conclude that the project is a failure, and I put the book back on the shelf, largely empty.

Some months later, I grow very ill and die. When I approach final judgement, there is an angel fully decked in white and exuding glory, sitting at a desk with a large book. I tell him my name and he checks the book but declares I am not listed. As he peruses the book, lots of small slips of paper tumble out and onto the floor beneath the table, where ugly little demons quickly gather them up and start running away with them. Curious, I ask about the book and what's happening, and the angel replies that it is the book of life, and at birth, the name of every individual goes into it and remains there while they live. But when they die, the names of those who did not hold on to what's in the good book are released from the book of life each time it is opened. And he demonstrates again by opening the book. Without shaking it, out come all kinds of little strips of paper that again, the ugly little demons under the table eagerly gather up. "Your name is among those that just fell," the angel informs me, "and one of these little fellows will now take you to your final destination."

Reunion

I am preparing to attend my first high school reunion after having missed several, and as they only take place once or twice every decade, a lot of time has passed since I saw any of my classmates. Shortly after graduation, I moved away and went to a college elsewhere, settled down and never returned to my hometown. So I expect this to be quite an interesting visit and anticipate a flood of memories to be activated as well. Just the thought of going has this effect, and my mind presents me with a vivid reenactment of early experiences.

It is very pleasant to relive them, many of which I'm remembering for the first time. I see classes and teachers and dances, coaches and games and big catches, lunchroom hijinks and elections, graduation and various other memories, and in all of it, I feel that I'm a very pristine and inspiring influence on others, someone who commands and infuses people with confidence and happiness.

In a way, it is like I am King Midas, turning to gold everything I touch. They were happy years, and even though much of that is usually credited to its being a time of youth, I feel that my presence increased that good feeling more profoundly as I played a role in daily life on a grand scale by being so involved in clubs, sports and student council. I was class president, captain of the baseball team and president of the key club.

So I fully expect my visit to be something like the return of the prodigal son for having been a no-show for so long.

When the day arrives, I keep a low profile at my hotel because I don't want anyone to recognize me too early and spread the news of my arrival. I decide to get there fashionably late to insure that everyone will be there when I make my entrance. When I do come through the doors, the party is in full swing, but I don't think it's very well attended, nor is the lighting very good. I remember our class being much larger, and I can't see anyone I know. I wait for people to approach me, but no one does. So I go up to people, look at their badges, try to remember them, and even if I don't, I say hello, giving them a moment to look at my name badge. But I find that my name doesn't do much for them, and they're not much interested in talking to me. Some see my name and abruptly walk away.

Later on, I see a neighbor with whom I was not very close, the only person I'd recognized but had been avoiding, and I just go up to find out what's going on, to ask where some faces that I haven't seen may be. To my great sadness, he relates to me that many people I know are dead, very tragically in many instances. Also, my closest friends' lives were ruined in other ways. He goes on and on until he finally just comes out and says that I thought I was some big deal with a huge entourage, but he says that the majority of people hated me for how I treated them, and eventually what went around came around, and that every life I touched turned to garbage after I left and that he expected mine had too.

Turned to Stone

It had been a long time since I'd been to church, and I dreaded mentioning it to my wife because I knew she would insist I follow through. I planned on working late Saturday night, and I couldn't promise I'd feel up to it in the early morning, but I honestly wanted to go, so I asked her to set the alarm for me.

Usually the alarm wakes and forces me to get out of bed to turn it off, but I later learned my wife heard it first and shut if off before it woke me. Fifteen minutes later, she asked if I was planning to get up, and I thought the alarm had yet to go off, so I stayed in bed to snooze a little and wait for it to sound. A few minutes later, my wife came in, her hair spread out in snakes, ordering me out of bed, that there was no time to waste.

My son was still sleeping downstairs, and she'd done something similar to him. She'd woken him up, and he asked for five more minutes. She came back twenty minutes later, hair up in snakes accusing him of oversleeping. He and I gathered in the kitchen, and I handed him a plate to use as a shield. "Don't look directly at her," I said. "Look only at her reflection in the plate."

We dressed quickly and, and I cut a banana in two and gave my son his half with the peel still on it. We took our plates and bananas to the car, and she got in the back seat. It was then that I realized I'd forgotten my coffee, so without saying anything, I went back into the house to get it. When I returned, one of the snakes bit me on the arm, but fortunately I was wearing a horsehide leather jacket, and the fangs did not go through to break my skin.

When we arrived in church, I picked up a chunk of coffee cake in the hallway and took it into the sanctuary. Before I could take a bite, I heard a loud hissing noise, and I knew without looking what it meant. She did not want me eating in church. So I took it to the hallway and gobbled it down, then returned, still not looking at her, and listened to music until the snakes turned back into a nice hairdo. Meanwhile my son went to Sunday School, and as the service started, I set the coffee thermos on the floor, and my wife inadvertently kicked it over. I cursed, and that did it. One of the snakes bit me on the neck, and as I grabbed the spot where the fangs broke the skin, I looked at her. Her eyes were glowing in rage, and I turned to stone right there.

I can still see and hear everything even though I am now just a statue in my church. I see my wife come in every Sunday with my son who looks up to me with a tear in his eye. After the incident, she donated me to the church, and I was further embellished with plaster to shape my outer appearance. They added robes and a beard, then painted me up to represent St. Stephen reacting to being struck with a rock at his neck when he was stoned by the people. My wife is very proud of me now, but every time she passes me, I know what she is thinking; that I should have gotten ready sooner and kept my mouth shut in church.

The Ticket

I'm supposed to meet my wife at the bus to go to a show with a large group, and I'm in a large building gathering up my school books in an otherwise empty classroom. When I'm finished collecting what I need, I go out the door and make my way through long hallways and concourses, finally arriving at the bus at exactly eight o'clock. Everyone's in a waiting room about to board, and after I say hello to my wife, I realize I've left my ticket behind in the classroom. My wife says they may allow me to go on without it, and I ask the bus driver if that is true. He tells me I should go back for the ticket and indicates they will wait for my return. My wife then criticizes me for not arriving earlier, chiding me that I could have more easily succeeded in doing this without it being a disruption for everyone else. I just grumble that she always finds a way to make me feel bad, and with that, I leave the waiting room to make my way back to retrieve my ticket.

When I enter the building, I am rushing and lose my sense of the surroundings, which have become somewhat unfamiliar to me. There are extremely long hallways and staircases. In my haste, I reach a junction on the second floor where there are two stairways, each leading into a long hallway, at which point I take the further stairway before realizing that the other would have saved time; and so I find myself going down long hallways and having to retrace my steps and taking the other route. At another moment, I go through a door and find myself in the open area of the outside quad surrounded by all the buildings. As I cross over a path that has been partially overturned, likely by students playing a prank, I stoop to make minor reparations and realize by doing so I am only adding precious minutes to the journey.

So I leave the damage as it is and rush across the lawn, which is muddy and slowing me down. At times, I have to stop and clean the bottom of my shoes of the clay collecting in thick globs. I think back to the bus and wonder how it's possible the driver could still be waiting for me. He must have given up on me by now, or maybe my wife is trying to convince him I will be along momentarily. I fear it must have left or be on the verge of leaving, so I try to quicken my step, but the stress of hurrying and worrying has put me out of breath, and I find I am going so slowly that I'm having to pull myself along by grabbing hold of the carpet on the floor, the lockers or anything else I can get my fingers on, but it doesn't seem to be helping.

All the while, still distant from the room with the ticket, I'm feeling out of breath and heavier and heavier as I'm filled with a sense that the bus could no longer be waiting, or if it is, that it certainly will not be there at the time I eventually return. I look at a clock and see it is already ten minutes after eight so I can't see how I could possibly make it back before eight twenty. If I'd only arrived at the bus earlier the first time, like my wife said, I'd have been in much better shape, and as I claw my way along, getting weaker and weaker, I know wherever she is, she is driving my life, always at the ready to punch my ticket to hell.

Apple Orchard

My mother had a beautiful apple orchard, and when I was little, she would let me play there, but as I grew older, she increased restrictions on me until she forbade that I should linger in the grove, saying she feared that I would damage the crop. Despite my earnest promises that I would do nothing to harm her precious garden, I was only allowed to be there under her watchful eye, though each day I had to cross the orchard to leave the property.

As I came of age, I had already started my own apple grove adjacent to hers, and despite the fact that I had my own development and interests, there was no end to her haranguing whenever I went to work in my orchard. She claimed I was making a path, and was insulted when I wondered why her worries previously had always been about trees and apples, and now it was about the very ground itself. As there was no way to appease her, I finally moved off her property and onto my own, which was a great benefit to me as I no longer had to listen to her constant belligerence regarding what belonged to her.

Some years later, she died, and I inherited the orchard and the house that was hers. The house was better, so I moved there and took the fence down and combined the groves, making them one. But to this very day, whenever I leave the house and cross the grove, until I reach the younger trees, I feel her wrath in every branch and apple and wish there was some way I could let it all go. I let people come in to gather what they will, and though they say the pies they make from them are sweet, to me they're rotten before they hit the ground.

The Painting

I am a painting that my wife loves. She sees something in it that I really cannot see myself, so I honestly can't describe the exact subject matter of the canvas, but since I know that I am in it, within the frames as I can feel her hands on my shoulders when she holds the painting, and by the way she stands before me and looks at me, I am guessing I am life-size but only a torso as I also can't feel anything below my legs. In this strange confinement, I have little to do but let time pass between "noticings" as I call them, moments when she pays some attention to me. These are generally affectionate, though there have been times she has derided me, but never my creator.

No, she has the utmost respect for the skill and technique, even genius that rendered me, but as for myself, I don't feel particularly gifted or filled with anything deserving of such notice, but I am grateful for having come to sense what I'm about through frequent contact with her. My whole sense of self seems bound up in what she makes of me though I am by no means anything so significant within myself by my own reckoning. Still, I don't convey this. I am tolerant and steadfast to provide what my creator intended, holding the pose as it were, that was given me, which my wife likes so much that she even carries me to bed with her and sets me on my side so that I will be there when she rolls over in my direction and faces me. It is from this position that I learned much of my status and form in the cosmos, from the way that she holds me and speaks to me.

She is tender and kind, and I suppose I feel I do not deserve such love and consideration, but I guess the purpose of a painting is that it be viewed and provide something for the viewer, so I try not to diminish that experience for her. And yet recently in the middle of the night, when she held me by the sides of my frame, though I was sideways in bed, I felt as if she were trying to hold me up in the sunlight and wake me, to have me be more than what I am, which I know I can never be. She dwelled on me for a long time, much longer than usual, to a point that I became much more conscious of myself than ever before. I think it was so much that I experienced a sense of "self-consciousness," not of awareness but embarrassment, and that as she moved forward in the darkness to kiss me I was for the first time able to actually move my head in the pigment to avoid her lips, and she could not tell that I had done this because it was so dark, and the surface of the painting is much the same, so she would not know the background from my forehead or lips.

Since then, I have learned to move even more. I am able to turn my head around almost straight back so while she thinks she is kissing me, it's really the back of my head, or perhaps it's all the same to her since I'm just a painting, after all. But in being able to move, I have this completely new sense of having evolved to a point where I can react within my environment even if I cannot ultimately escape it, and even if I signal nothing but what my creator intended, and even though it is sad that my own reactions are not consistent and parallel with those of my admirer, it feels like a great step for me to react in a way of my own choosing, and if I were a painting of Christ or His mother and were to shed a tear, it would be heralded as a miracle. So now as she adores me in the dark, I wriggle my way slightly to avoid her affection more as a technicality because she loves the painting, but to me, as the whole situation stands, it is more just a sad tale of a painting that spends far less time on the wall than it should, and one that would turn around and face the wall like a punished child if only it could.

The Needle

I am at the doctor complaining about everything as I have been very depressed. He listens intently, trying to make me sum everything up into a single phrase. I tell him I don't think I can do that as each issue has its own associated pain, but he says in such cases any remedy given for, say, the finger, would also influence the toe since the medicine goes into the same body. So I ask for time to think about it and go home where I find that looking at everything closely from the vantage point of trying to ascertain a general sense of a condition, my interest seems to have been sucked out of what I used to enjoy. No matter what task it is that I try to do, it appears to be without any interest at all for me, which again I blame on my depression, but looking at it, conscious of it, it all seems just so much worse than even I had thought it was before going to the doctor.

Within a few days, I am feeling awful and think I have a working phrase that describes my condition, so I return to the doctor and tell him that I believe I'm just sick and tired of planet Earth. The doctor puts me through a few basic reflex tests and checks my ears and eyes. As he's washing his hands, he declares that I'm a perfect candidate for the "Platinum Needle," and that it will cure my condition.

My first question is whether the doctor agrees with my conclusion that I'm tired of the planet, and he just says that my own assessment has to be given considerable weight in any analysis, for after all, it is my life we're talking about, and I'm as good a judge if not a better one than even he could be. My next question is about the platinum needle, for I already can feel the goodness coming from it even if I haven't heard any of the music it will play. I'd always used diamond needles, but they ended up ruining my music collection because I could never tell when they had worn out. Platinum being a hard yet non-tarnishing metal makes a lot of sense, as does vinyl, which is renowned for the quality of sound one experiences, so it is clearly a magical combination, one that I'm surprised I haven't heard of before.

But given my depression, much of it stemming from all of the attention paid to gadgetry and electronics, which makes people focus on other things more than people and life itself, I am not surprised to learn about a technological advancement improving something old by the additional element of something new. I have been tuning everything out, so I would have missed or ignored news on that. But I find the idea exciting, so I say I am looking forward to it, and the nurse prepares me by having me lie down on a comfortable cot. She turns on some music, and it is scratch free, very pretty and calming. I realize I haven't listened to music in quite a while, and that I might feel a whole lot differently in my life if I would only include it, so I'm happy everything has worked out along these lines for what I am realizing.

Just as I am experiencing reaching this conclusion, the doctor walks over, wipes my arm with a cotton ball wet with rubbing alcohol and gives me a shot. Immediately I begin to feel weak and ask what he has given me. He explains it is a death shot from a platinum needle, which will leave no metallic trace, and that my death will not be on him. "My death!?" I yell. "I don't want to die!"

"Well, but when you said you were tired of the planet, you invoked the platinum needle, which represents a rare and valuable judgement on one who thinks he's so much better than everyone else that he can take something like life so lightly as to waste away in emotional ineptitude. As you come full circle in a life that clearly started with a silver spoon in your mouth, a platinum needle is actually the perfect musical finish that ends your arrogant concerto in a full measure of what you so richly deserve, a moment of silence, because you failed to grasp the importance of every moment."

As my eyes started to close for good, I thought of all the many good things I would miss, and things I would never see, but I especially thought of the music, and it bothered me not to know the name of the wonderful, unfamiliar piece I was hearing for the first and last time. Silence indeed! That piece was blasting loud and full, and I'm pretty sure it was a symphony, not a concerto, but I got the point.

Glasses

I'm visiting with my father who is in ill health, and my brother arrives to say hello. As I'm speaking to my father, my brother is busying himself around the room arranging things, but he spends an inordinate amount of time on my father's several pairs of reading glasses, cleaning them with spray and tissue. He wipes each lens far beyond what it needs, and it looks as if he's grinding a new prescription or that he believes the amount of cleaning corresponds to the duration the lenses will repel grime. When he finishes each pair, he sets them down on the table next to my father. My brother continues to bustle while my father and I talk, and at one point my father mentions a newspaper article and reaches down near his feet on the bed to snatch the paper, then grabs a pair of reading glasses from the table, taking them up by the lenses rather than the temples. My brother takes them away and hands my father a different set, then re-cleans the lenses of the ones my father had just smudged.

Later on, when I am alone with my brother, having coffee in a restaurant, I try to talk about my father's condition, his future and my worries, but my brother keeps festering on the glasses. He cannot understand how he lets them get so dirty. He says that every time he comes to visit, he finds my father in a bed or chair staring out from behind lenses covered with fingerprints. He can't get over how lazy and unconcerned my father is to let the lenses get so dirty, then not care enough to clean them. While he is telling me about this, he is flossing his teeth, followed by using a toothpick, then going back to flossing all over again. I ask what he is doing, and he explains that he had a bad experience with his gums from not taking care of his teeth for many years, and now he cleans his teeth whenever he has a chance. He also explains that he uses a strong mouthwash and holds it in his mouth for the duration of an entire morning shower in order to kill every germ in his mouth.

But I see something else in his eyes. I see a desire to dip each tooth-pick in poison and stick me with them. I sense while he's flossing and the bits of spit are flying out with each snap that he'd really like to wind the floss around my neck and hang me up with it. I've never seen such contained fury. So I excuse myself and go the men's room for a moment to distance myself from him. I've never really liked it when people perform acts of personal hygiene in public. As I'm washing my hands, I happen to look in the mirror and see that my glasses have a few light smudges on them, nothing that would demand an immediate cleaning, but I suddenly understand my tacit death sentence.

The Flames

As I am born, my grandfather lights a candle and places it on the table next to my mother's bed. He holds me in his arms and declares he never felt such warmth in such a small body, and by comparison he feels quite cold. Through that humid night and as the sun rises and makes the morning very hot, he complains of chills. As he hands me off to my father, he bumps the candle, and it falls to the floor and starts a fire under a table. My father hands me off to my mother, and rushes to extinguish the flames. My mother and I are helpless, but it is more a big scare than anything as he has no trouble putting out the fire.

I've been told that story many times, and one of my greatest regrets is that I never got to meet my grandfather. He died within weeks of my birth in what was one of the hottest summers on record. Like many old people, he didn't seem to feel the heat. During the winter after I turned five years old, I remember my mother told me in front of a warm fire in the fireplace how he would sleep under the blankets with windows closed in a room without air conditioning and not be bothered by it in the least. But it was the life in him when he was younger that made me wish that I had met him. Everyone had stories about his fantastic personality, about how much he cared for others, how warm he was, and how he made everyone laugh. From an early age, I wanted to be like him.

But something happened that night when he held me and knocked over the candle. Something serious inside him became a clear manifestation. The day of my birth was the beginning of the end for him, and so I have always felt a strange connection to him. Every year on my birthday, I've gone outside in the dark to sit by myself and reflect on my life, and he always comes to mind. On the day I turned twenty-one and became a man, my father told me that a small fire had started in the old house where I was born. It was very similar to the fire he'd put out the night I was born, but the current residents of the house were somehow unable to handle it, and it very quickly engulfed the house. I found this very strange news indeed and thought about this a great deal. When I went out with friends that night, even though I had intended that it would be the most festive evening of my life, with lots of drinking and dancing, my friends sensed something was wrong, that I was somewhat withdrawn. It was terribly hot that night, but as we were leaving, I felt a cool breeze even before we got into the convertible. On such nights, it's normal to feel a certain coolness in the air especially when driving through the forest, but I felt it before we got into the car, and I wanted to put the top up on the car, but I was voted down by my friends who couldn't believe I'd even suggest such an idea. It was actually a very pleasant drive home, and I didn't think much more about it.

Around the time I turned thirty, as I sat in my backyard with my wife and children looking at the stars, I saw a dim glow on the horizon that I'd never seen before. I felt cool and asked my wife to get me a sweater. She was always sympathetic and agreed that the air was a little cool that night, but she didn't bring a sweater or blanket for herself. Later I saw on the news that there was a forest fire hundreds of miles away, and though it was impossible that I could have seen it from such a distance, the thought had occurred to me that it might be a fire.

When I turned fifty, the blaze was obvious on the horizon, and my wife knew that I couldn't sit out back without a blanket and sweater even on what seemed a hot night for everyone else. I had to install special light blocking curtains in the bedroom because the constant flickering of the fire bothered me. To me, it was the fire that had started in my old homestead when I was twenty-one.

Actually, I even thought perhaps the candle my grandfather had tipped over had ignited something in the flooring, which smoldered there as an ember taking only the molecule or two of oxygen it needed to stay alive. As microbes thrive under the ice in the arctic for thousands of years, so the fire started on the night of my birth grew and crossed thousands of miles to engulf me, and when it finally reached my house, it found me a cold old man, exactly like my grandfather. I remember looking out the window on the night my grandson was born, somewhat terrified but also relieved to see burning branches crashing down in sparks on the lawn, the air filled with embers. My wife was afraid the way I bundled up, but in respect for family tradition, I lit a candle and placed it next to my daughter on the nightstand. I held my grandson and found him very warm, and I was very careful not to knock the candle down. But even so, I still felt an increase in the chills from that point going forward.

But I actually weathered the firestorm better than my own grandfather. The flames' arrival slowed them down a bit. I just had a way of making them wait, and it's amazing how such a large firestorm lapping at the very foundations of one's life can also go into a smoldering mode and go no further. I enjoyed many years and was able to get to know my grandson, and I hope at least that he will not have the same regret that I had for not knowing my grandfather. But finally the day came. I felt exceedingly cold and knew it was my time, at which point the fire came in and took me. And when I died, everyone told stories of how warm and wonderful I was in life, and though he will not need it for a while, I'm confident my grandson will treasure the sweater that I left him in my will.

Back Seat

I'm in the back seat of my friend's car. He is driving me somewhere. He's an alcoholic who's been in and out of prison for driving while intoxicated. He's clearly drunk at the moment, and he has a bottle in the front seat that he won't stop drinking from despite my objections from the back seat. He just laughs and says it's not a problem, not to worry, we'll get there. I'm not even sure where he's taking me anymore.

We started out from his house going toward town, but now we're way beyond the city limits from what I can tell, and frankly I can't see much because he fills so much of the front seat that he almost completely obstructs my view. I can't seem to get a word in as he keeps insisting he has it under control and that he's been my driver for years and I shouldn't be yapping at him but letting him do his job. It is then that I start trying to think back, and I realize that I can't remember a time when I went anywhere that he wasn't at the wheel. I'm not sure how I could have blocked it all out, but the ride he's giving me even at the moment is certainly one I'd like to forget.

He's not staying in his lane or even on the road. He drives onto the median almost to the opposite lanes of traffic, and just before getting there, he lets out a big laugh and goes back to our side of the road as if suddenly realizing what he is doing. Or maybe he is just doing it to get a rise out of me. Either way, I try to think of some way to get rid of him, to fire him if he is working for me as my driver, but as I look around in the back seat, everything I own is here. It's actually a rather huge vehicle. I thought it was a car, but I think it's actually a trailer.

As I look around, I see it's my house. My wife is here, and so are my children. She looks at me as if detecting something is wrong. I smile and try to exude confidence. I can see out the window across the street to my neighbor's house, but then as I look in front of me, there is a car seat with my alcoholic friend sitting at the wheel driving me. I do not know how it can be his car and yet my house, but somehow I know it to be true. Each time I try to deal with it, to try to understand it, he goes off the road and skirts along the ditch almost to the point of going into it but not quite, shaking those thoughts out of me from fear. I beg him to be careful, and he tells me not to worry and takes another huge swig from his bottle.

As much as I feel compelled to sit and monitor what he's doing, it becomes increasingly obvious that I have no control, so I go back into my house and do the best I can to block access to the passenger area. I see my wife has made dinner, and when I sit down, she asks about my day. I tell her I made a lot of progress as she knows how I hate to stand still.

Clouds

One night when my uncle is visiting, I suggest we go downtown to a club at the top of a skyscraper. He agrees, and so I drive him into the city and park in a garage next to the tower. Looking up as we enter, the antennae are obscured by clouds, and the top of the building looks like it's skewing a pillow. The clouds are quite low, but below the top few floors, it is clear. After an ear-popping elevator ride up more than a hundred stories, we are seated next to a window.

To our delight, we are sitting exactly at the level of the bottom of the clouds. It is like being on a boat in a clear glass of water where you can look down and see the bottom of the glass, but dancing all around, and sometimes dipping below you and engulfing you, a huge dollop of whipped cream or foam is floating on top all around you.

From above, as the clouds dip down, it must look like the slender buildings are peeking through the clouds like serpents from time to time, only to retreat and disappear into the whiteness.

So we sit there mesmerized as the cloud layer rides the air as if it were the ocean. The cloud level shifts constantly in the waves of wind, and one moment we cannot see a thing except a white fog, and the next the lights of the street so far below are clear and bright.

It is difficult under these circumstances for either one of us to have a conversation. People travel thousands of miles to witness a volcanic eruption or an eclipse, and this has our attention in much the same way. We become completely involved in the experience, and without a word, share an experience so compelling that we feel singled out as witnesses to this perfect moment. People would be lining up if such events were reported and realized for their beauty, but they are not even predicable, nor are they likely to last long enough for anyone to rush up in the hope of seeing it. It really is rather like the foam of a soda that dissipates quickly, and there is no known way of shaking it up to recreate the effect.

We lose track of the time and have a few drinks as we watch the display. Finally the clouds dip lower and totally obscure the streets below. We wait a while, hoping it will lift, but we realize it is time to go, so without having said more than a few words together, we get up and leave. On the ride home, we are generally quiet except for the occasional word of praise followed by laughter brought on by having been fortunate enough to experience a true wonder of nature.

The next day, my uncle flew home. A week later, I received a card where he thanked me for taking him to the top of the tower. A few days after that, I missed his phone call but he left a message that he would call back. I thought of calling him back, but I got busy, and besides, he said in his message that he would call me again.

Then I received word that he died, and I've always wondered about his call. It sits like a cloud in my mind, hovering sometimes just above where I can see, and quite often dipping down and filling my head with vague semblances born of every attempt I make to discover what cannot be ascertained.

Aged to Perfection

When I was fifty, I brewed a style of beer known as Imperial Stout. What intrigued me about it was a statement in the recipe that indicated it ages to perfection in thirty years, though it can certainly be imbibed earlier than that. When I was finished bottling the batch, there were two cases, plus an extra bottle or two, which I tucked away in the cool environment of a basement closet. About a month later, I opened one of the extras and tried it. Like a successful liftoff of a rocket from the launch pad, everything about it was good. Now the long waiting period was just beginning.

About three years later, there was a block party where everyone brought their own food and beverages. Late in the evening, someone asked me about my home brewing, and I said I had a batch of Imperial Stout that was already one tenth of the way to perfection. When I explained the situation, several men talked me into going home and bringing back a six pack. It was actually very good at that point, marvelous in fact, and I wondered how it could get any better.

I let it sit again after that, and I didn't serve any until my sixtieth birthday as it seemed appropriate to see what it tasted like after a full ten years, though that was only a third of the way to a fully-aged brew. After the toast and celebration, another six bottles were gone, but there was still another case and half left for the next twenty years of waiting.

Five years later, my wife surprised me with a party, and my son took the liberty of bringing another six-pack of my famous Imperial Stout out of storage for the occasion. Again, it was wonderful to sample it, and I could still make comparisons to the few other times I had tried it along the way, and I could honestly say it was still improving in the bottle.

At the age of seventy, when I went to retrieve a couple of bottles to see how it tasted after twenty years, there were only fourteen bottles left. I could not remember having any or giving any away. My wife said she vaguely recalled something about my giving my son permission to take some for a special occasion, but I had totally forgotten. I decided I would have to be more careful with it, but it was so special to have a beer that was still good after twenty years that I would give away a bottle at a time to old friends on the occasions of milestone birthdays and such. I lost track of the original intent to go the distance, and by the time I was seventy five, there was only one bottle left, which I put away for five long years, determined that I would only have it after the full thirty years if I made it that long myself.

When I reached my eightieth birthday, I didn't open it because it still had six months to go. That took will power. Finally, it is a full thirty years old. I take that last bottle of Imperial Stout and make careful preparations with a friend present to open and sample this last bottle. When the cap comes off, we take turns sniffing the fragrance of a fully-matured, thirty-year-old brew. I then pour it out into two cups, after which we toast to long life, and et cetera. Then we tilt the cups to our mouths so the liquid just touches our lips. We instantly recognize how wonderfully it has aged. My last living friend agrees that it is perfect, and all we keep saying as we sip it slowly is that I should have made more.

The Casting of Stones

I liked skipping stones as a child, and sometimes I'd deliberately throw at a duck in the water, and father told me every stone I threw would one day boomerang in one way or another and nail me. We used to watch massive flocks migrating south for the winter, and years later, I hardly see but a few on rare occasions. In those early days, I used to throw whole handfuls of rocks heavenward with obviously no chance of hitting anything, but my father reminded me that some day those stones would return in bunches.

Lately I've been having lots of dreams where I feel like each one is a kind of stone I threw coming back to get me. At first, there were only a few, and now they come in clusters. Throughout the night, I'm waking up from nightmares and having trouble going back to sleep. I have recorded many of these dreams in the hope that someone might find something in them to explain the connection to the casting of stones and why I am being literally pummeled. My father said that everyone gets back everything they do, that it isn't just in stones, but in words, and that in the end it all evens out. I asked him then why the birds have disappeared because they haven't done anything, and he said that through the ages though it evens out for an individual in ways one cannot comprehend, the earth itself is being picked apart, literally ground up into stones due to the increase in population, and the result is that what used to be one giant stone in the heavens is slowly becoming just a pile of rubble. The animals were the first to go. Now they haunt us in our dreams. Now we just throw stones at one another in word and deed. Each day we find new ways to deliver handfuls of stones at everyone we see, and each night we toss and turn as the stones return in the form of unpleasant dreams. The process has speeded up, and soon we all will turn to dust in the same way that we're grinding down the earth.

Last night I dreamed that an astronomer discovered a huge asteroid speeding straight for earth and that it would destroy the planet and kill every living thing on it. The information was kept from the public, and we were only told about it when it was just an hour away. In the dream, everyone started running around in a panic, but I was calm. To me it was one big stone coming back to me, a collection of every stone I'd ever thrown in one big ball. Everyone thought I was crazy, but it made me laugh, and it didn't occur to me at the time that I might be dreaming. I took it very seriously, but I laughed, and when the asteroid hit and woke me up, I felt as if I'd slept like a baby.

Migration

I am a bird in flight with a strong sense that I know where I'm going even though I'm flying with thousands of my kind. Why, if they were all to suddenly turn left, I would still feel the urge to continue on my current flight path, and I would not go with them. But we seem to all share the same sense of which way to go, and we even have a collective idea of where to set down to rest and when to start flying again.

Now I am flying back home after months of good rest in a very nice warm region. I might have thought it was getting very cool before we left, but I didn't stay long enough to find out. Now in coming back, it's almost like the way I left it, only the trees are bare, though they look like they are turning green again. It looks like something happened, but I'm not sure what. I do notice that there are dwellings around what used to be our pond, and though we land there for a while, it isn't long before some beings come out and disturb us, so we fly off in order to find a new spot.

Now it is feeling cool again like before, and I feel a strong urge to go back to that wonderful place so far away, and it seems thousands of others feel the same way about it. Again we are in flight, and again we arrive in this very nice region. I wonder why I don't just stay here, but after a very nice visit, I feel the urge to return home, and again take flight with thousands of my companions, and again, on returning, I notice there are more dwellings than before, and we have to find new places of solitude.

Now it is a long time since I made my first flight, and now there are not so many of us. The dwellings are everywhere it seems, and now they even surround what used to be our rest areas. Even the area where we loved to visit is no longer the same. Something has happened that we no longer fill the skies when we fly. Last time I flew, I recall there were only ten of us together, and going back there are seven. Not only that, but there were always other groups to join, and now we don't see anyone else for days.

I am feeling more tired now, and something tells me this might be my last trip. There have been some young ones that I hoped would follow me, but they stayed behind the first time as they had nobody to lead them, and now they do not understand that to follow would mean a wonderful visit to a great place. Well, it used to mean something like that. I can't say I blame them for staying, but I cannot remain. The urge to fly is so great, and now I am flying over what looks like the great resting area.

There are only four of us this time, and we are alone in our journey. I have seen none of our kind anywhere. Now as I look down at the great resting area, I hear something. Explosions of some kind. My friend to my right wing suddenly falls. I see. They are shooting at us from below. I remember they used to do that when there were thousands of us, and I had little fear. I don't recall ever being close to anyone who was hit, but now a second friend is falling.

Now there are only two of us. I'm looking for our shadows on the ground. The first time I made this journey, we were like a cloud, and I looked for glints of light below. Now I see something like that, but they are the bursts from guns, and the great shadow lies beneath me, and the sun is blinding as I squint to see my feathers slowly coming down after me.

The Black Hand

I am a key participant in a ritual that is important in our culture, celebrated annually, and I am in the final stage of the procession accompanying a lady who is more like a sybil than an ordinary dignitary, highly regarded for her sacred trust as keeper of the final words of respect to be paid from her lips when we're finished coming down these last several flights of stairs at the pace prescribed over the loud speakers as we descend. She is highly regarded, and I am her counterpart. We take the stairs slowly, one at a time, our arms intertwined as prescribed by design, according to a long tradition. I'm wearing black gloves. She has nothing over her hands, but they are elegant like those of an artist. They are wrinkled as she is very old, yet she is leading this dance.

The ceremony awaits, approaching quickly. On the last flight, the timing is off, so the pace changes to quicken our step. We begin to fly down, it seems. Our legs go so fast over stairs thick and wide, but she takes them so dextrously that I'm amazed how supple she is. I can just keep up, and when we get out into the open ballroom, she begins to make the incantation, to say the grace as it were, for all those present, now bowing their heads in unison for this blessing, which is an essential part of our going forward through the next year.

But as she speaks, at the windows and on verandas above in nearby buildings where the citizens are invited to watch, there are any number of disturbances. Some people are laughing. Others are having loud conversations. The animals of some are making loud, unpleasant noises, all of it disruptive to the proceedings. Our sybil makes no note of it, but continues through her words faithfully and flawlessly, and as she does so, I do my part, fulfill my role by scanning and marking each and every transgression for follow-up as I must, for they are to be purged, or I am not The Black Hand in all of this.

The Messages

I am the bearer of bad news, and my satchel is full today, just like every other day, overflowing with messages of a terrible truth that will ruin not just the days but the lives of many who will open their doors to me to receive them. Over the years, my attitude about this job has evolved. I started out hating it. I didn't know how to approach people. They always had a quizzical, expectant and friendly look on their faces. I hated to shatter that illusion and become the messenger they wanted to kill. I mean, it never had anything to do with me. I always felt like I was one of them, but the deep and sorrowful look that I would give them on handing over the bad news never sat well with them, at least as far as I could do some kind of intuitive subtraction and differentiate their reaction to me from the terrible news they had just received. One might think they wouldn't care a bit about me, but the door slamming was just the beginning in many cases. I wouldn't be halfway from the door to the sidewalk before the door would open again, and things would start flying at me, anything they could get their hands on. I've even had a few people take shots at me with guns, but I usually picked out who those would be when they would say, "Wait here a moment." As soon as I heard that, I started running.

But those were the early years. I could say that I grew a thicker skin because I was doing this all day long every day, but then there were sometimes the people I knew personally. It seemed like as soon as I had figured out how to keep the reality of my job in the back of my mind, all the sudden I'd be looking into the eyes of a dear friend and then giving them bad news. That was very hard for me.

But what changed somewhere along the way was that I made a kind of transformation of the news itself. I realized I wasn't being forced to deliver it in the basic form of a set of facts, which had never gone down well. I could sugar coat it any way I pleased. So I would take each message individually and begin to massage it before I would even get to the door. By the time I got there, I would have something a bit better to say, something realistic and terrible, but they might not see it right away. I'd get a delighted response, then hear screaming when I was halfway down the street. It wasn't what I wanted, but it was easier to deal with that way.

That was just one stage, and I should say that I am only one carrier. There are many like me, some better and more experienced, some brutal and cold, and I am also just anybody who at some point becomes the recipient of bad news.

The day it came for me, I was just getting ready to go out and do my own job. What happened was I just got it as I had been giving it, but it felt colder, more brutal, with no caring whatsoever. I even suspected the delivery person enjoyed the moment, and I thought of doing something to retaliate, but my own experience kicked in a bit, and in my heart, I forgave the messenger. I received even more bad news shortly thereafter, and this time I found myself having to comfort the delivery person who was shaken up by the ordeal. It was a very strange twist to the experience, but this was a peculiarly empathetic delivery person.

It took me a while to get back on the job. I found myself leaving messages in mailboxes or on the doorknob. I didn't even want to deal with people. It took a long time before I could face people, but the experiences gave me a growth spurt of sorts, and I was able to evaluate my approach compared to how I would want to be treated.

As a result, I now love my job. I have found a way to rewrite the bad news into a form where there is understanding and no backlash afterwards. Basically, my approach is as if I were naked, completely nude, with no pretensions of any kind, and I let them know the full truth, which is to say that there is total balance in the reporting. By the time I leave them with the thought that they are going to die, for example, and nothing can be done about it, they have hope for something greater because they have experienced a heightened sensation somewhere in my words. I used to want to kill myself doing this job. Now I live for others and think of it as just delivering what has to be said, and even if it's bad news, they allow me to console them in a shared sense of pain.

A Loft

I have taken refuge in what I thought was the safest place to conceal my most secret thoughts, a kind of barn hidden in the deepest woods. I am crouching in the loft, which seems like a safe place except that it is not very deep, more like a catwalk, and it is so cold that my breath is visible and could give me away. Those that seek me are nearby, which has always been the case to some extent, but lately I have made mistakes due to my having grown slightly fatigued by the cat and mouse game, and these lazy oversights have only brought them closer, and I fear they will soon be upon me.

Beneath me, on the floor of the barn, covered in hay, is everything they wish to find. I have been careful over the years to place new items into the arrangement in such a way as to camouflage the entirety of it, but from my vantage point, it is all so obvious that the "X" marking the spot where the treasure lies could not be more pronounced.

Suddenly I hear them coming. They're at the door, and it strikes me that the one thing I can do is to call more attention to myself by jumping down. In the loft, I appear to be hiding something, and it will call attention to everything, give them cause to search the place. I'm sure they have shovels with them and will tear the place apart. But if they find me casually seated in the open area, it might appear that I am merely situated along a route somewhere between their starting point and the end point where I've tucked away what has them looking for me in the first place. If this works, they will simply take me out for questioning as they always do, which will also render this location an innocuous, random establishment where I happen to have stopped for a rest. Along the road leading here, there are thousands of such places, and so many instances of false arrest that I cannot count them. I have also ensured that if I can get past this moment, there are plenty of false leads and hideouts going forward to keep them busy for years, allowing me to continue to use this place with impunity, but I must make my move quickly.

Just as the door starts to open, I make my leap, landing on the top of the totally hidden construct just as I'd hoped, with legs casually crossed so as to appear innocent, otherwise engaged in my own thoughts so as to throw them completely off the scent. But something unexpected occurs. The ground on which my life's work sits is actually quite flexible if not buoyant. As I land on it, my weight sets in motion a kind of trampoline effect, throwing me back onto the catwalk and everything I've ever done up into the air where it remains aloft for ripe plucking. Aghast and unable to stop them, I watch as they bide their time cataloguing every last piece of the puzzle that makes me who I am, then carting it all away, leaving me empty in the confines of my own full exposure.

A Simple Truth

I feel myself floating upwards, and I realize that I have died. Soon my spirit comes face to face with the eternal Creator, and I am infused with great understanding. The meaning of life is all so simple that I could write it on a small piece of paper. I ask if it would be possible to have this message sent to Earth so as to help everyone, and to have it appear on television. I request to be allowed to deliver the message as well. The eternal spirit says He can do better than that, and all at once He turns me into a small piece of paper with the words describing the meaning of life infused on me. He explains that I will have no other power to reach people other than to deliver myself as a piece of paper, but He adds that I will appear on television. I am so pleased, and suddenly I feel myself falling from the sky back to Earth.

As I float and tumble in the winds, I find myself over a large city. There beneath me is some kind of facility that looks like a sports stadium. Yes, it is a baseball park. I drift in, slowly floating down until finally I land in the outfield on the warning track. At the same time I happen to look up and see myself on the giant video screen in the stands behind center field. Something in the game has just made the home fans angry, and it looks like I have been dropped out of the seats with lots of other paper and garbage that is now littering the field.

The message I have for the world is clear, but I am only in proximity and visible to one person who is an outfielder. He is positioned close to me, but I am still too small to notice, and now with the all the litter on the track, I do not stand out. I have no power to move, but the wind blows me over on my blank side. The umpires quickly call for the grounds crew to clean the outfield, and within a few minutes of my arrival, the TV shows someone stabbing me with a nail on a stick and putting me in a refuse bag destined for the dump.

Literary Wings

A friend of mine who has always had a superior, natural grasp of ideas and words has asked me to examine her most recent work, and as I pour over the recently handwritten pages, I am stunned with a combination of admiration and envy, a feeling of being whisked above the natural order of things where I can look down and see everything as it has been woven together, as a kind of fabric, only that there is a pool in the middle where I see my own reflection, and what I see I do not like. I don't like to compare our work, but I cannot help it. While she produces wings that fly over and reveal everything on a grand scale along with the underlying true nature of all things, I screw cheap metal components together into lifeless forms that have very little to offer in terms of overall functionality. My creations are well made in their own way, yet betray in every aspect that they are fabricated and full of flaws. By themselves, they are fine enough, but given a choice between the box that sits on the floor or the wings that fly above the world, anyone would choose the wings, and though it hurts, so do I.

What we have in common is that I don't take anything apart, though I certainly take it all in and see much of it as parts of a great whole. If anything, I simply fly over the fabric and occasionally stop over an area where I see some sign of stitching and try to reveal exactly what I see as the underlying design. My hope is that eventually one will come to understand that there is a kind of fabric that covers and underlies everything, and that it can be seen but neither taken apart nor repaired, at least not by me. What I do is more a witnessing than anything else. It's not judgement. It's simply observation.

But for me to even say what she creates is a cheap box that might hold wings, but does not help them fly or understand how they fly in any way. I am just left amazed, and by the time I finish reading the pamphlet of new works she has given me, I have surveyed my own life and know how small I am, and yet at the same time I feel somehow more enriched and capable of making better boxes, so it is with a firm sense of pride that I know her, that I close the folder and prepare to send praises and honest expectations, no, certainty, that these new works will do well once allowed to fly on their own, so to speak.

But a few days later, while I am in the midst of preparing my response, I hear the terrible, sad news that my friend has died. Of course I go to the wake and attend the funeral, and after a week of mourning I know a big part of me is gone. All I have left of her is this satchel of last papers, the culmination of her best work, that nobody knows about except for me. I have never admitted to being perfect nor completely honest, though I have strived in all ways to be the best person I can be. But as I read over her works a second time, there is a difference in how I am perceiving them. Strangely, I am looking at them as being mine, not that they were done by me, but that I own them. By possessing the only known copy, I find myself in the unique position of being able to steal the ideas though I know I cannot pass them off as my own. People would know they were hers. She has a distinct style. But I feel that I can use them as parts for my own creations, build them into my machines as it were, and rather than ending up with useless boxes, my new machines will have wings, and they will fly.

So I set out immediately to work and begin fashioning a typical housing, but somehow I am doing it much more carefully, more lovingly than I have ever done before. My own work has been taken up more than a notch I discover, and when I merge her wings into my own creations, a new entity emerges with its own distinct characteristics that could naturally be interpreted as an unexpected advancement of my own work, but not as a theft, though perhaps as being highly influenced by her work, which is fine with me as long as I get the ultimate credit.

As I finish assembling all of the works, which takes quite a long time, I finally have an amazing assemblage of beautiful flying machines, each a combination of wings and gondolas that will have no limit to the number of minds that can be carried to survey the fabric of life and what underlies everything. I have even imagined seeing myself in the reflecting pool, and it is a different person, that despite my having stolen these works, I have used them in a manner that I would like to think even she would not just condone and understand, but support and applaud.

Then comes the moment of launch, but when I release them, they do not fly. I cannot seem to get them off the ground. The wings are robust and strain to take flight, but not an inch of air is gained. I wait for a windy day, and they still cannot take off, but I do notice that there is some drifting in the sands, so I consider that perhaps the wings will best serve as sails. So I take these constructions to the reflecting pool and connect them into an armada, and standing in the largest one, I let go the anchor and find that they quickly begin to submerge, forcing me to jump ship.

As I watch them go under, I see that the gondolas and wings are adapting very well to the new environment, taking on a life of their own, working together as body and fins. Soon, they completely disappear from the surface, and it is not long before I hear reports that they have been seen flourishing in the great depths. But there has always been something of me in the pool, a species of life, and I feel these new sharks not just feeding on them in the deep, but ripping me apart from within where I stand.

Foul Friends

I am having trouble concentrating and cannot finish my work, so I visit a doctor who if rumors are true is a war criminal. After listening to my complaint, he takes out his pen and says he is writing a note to someone who can help me, who also has friends if I need more assistance than he can provide. After writing for a few seconds, he folds up the paper and tells me to eat it, then go home and take a nap. He give me a glass of water and watches as I swallow it, and per his orders I return home. By the time I get there, I am feeling terribly tired, and so I lay down on my bed as he told me and take a nap.

When I wake, there is a man sitting on a chair in my bedroom. He tells me he got the note from the doc and is at my service. He pours himself a drink and introduces himself as Duke. I show him my current project, and he sits right down and begins working with amazing alacrity. Within a few hours, he produces a finished result with the highest level of professionalism I have ever seen. I make a phone call, drive into the city and turn it in. I receive the highest praises and am rewarded with several new contracts, but by the time I get home, I have a splitting headache. My friend Duke writes a note and tells me to swallow it. He hands me a glass of water and watches as I down his note while drinking it. Within a few minutes, my headache has already improved, but I feel very tired and take a nap.

When I wake, there is another man sitting across from Duke. They are playing cards and drinking. Duke introduces his associate as King, and they tell me they have already looked over the new contracts I have received and will get started on them right away. There are many things to do, and these are not projects that anyone could complete quickly. So while they begin to start on the outlines, I reorganize a couple of rooms so that they can stay a while. A few weeks later, everything looks great, and I take what they have finished into the city and make very successful presentations, promising that I can have everything done within a few months. My clients find it hard to believe, but I receive a round of applause as I leave the meeting.

When I get back home, again I have a terrible headache, but neither Duke nor King are anywhere to be found. I thought they might provide some remedy, but I don't even know where they went.

An hour or so later, I am awakened by loud noises downstairs. It seems Duke and King have managed to make some friends after a night on the town and have brought the party home. I ask that they keep the volume down, and Duke approaches menacingly and declares that I should withdraw before something bad happens to me. I take his advice, but I don't like his tone. I decide that I will dismiss the two of them the next morning, but when I wake, they are hard at work and have already made good progress with the projects. But early in the evening, they go out again, and later bring the party back with them. This time King runs interference and tells me to mind my own business when I complain. When I wake the following morning they are hard at work, but at the same time they ignore me and do not wish to show me what they are working on.

That night, they don't bother to go out, but lots of people start showing up early, and by eight P.M. a raucous party to which I am not invited in my own house is in full swing. I know better than to say anything, but they both still manage to come into my room and demand that I be more quiet even though I am doing nothing, and the noise downstairs is so loud they couldn't possibly have heard me doing anything.

The next morning, I wake with a terrible headache and find the party is still going on. While they are busy, I sneak into the study and look over the projects to see what they have accomplished, but all I can find are doodles over my notes. I also find betting slips and my bankbook, which they have apparently been using to forge checks to finance their gambling. As I'm examining all of this, my headache has grown so bad that I feel I am going to be sick. I pass through the party and tell King and Duke directly that I wish them to leave. They laugh in my face and tell me to stand right there while they get their coats. As I stand there, they put them on and walk over to the door, watching me the whole time. As they open the door and step over the threshold outside, I feel terrible cramps and begin vomiting all over the floor. I double up and fall on the floor with horrendous abdominal pains. Then they step back inside, and I don't feel the pains anymore. Duke says he forgot his hat, and King says he left his scarf on the kitchen table. After retrieving these items, they again step outside just as I'm getting to my feet, and again I double over in pain and go down on my knees. As I look up, they are smiling at me, and then they ask if I would like to invite them back inside. As I nod, they return, but now they want me to clean up for them and bring them and their guests more food and drink. There's nothing I can do except comply.

A few weeks later, I have to phone and cancel my contracts. I have been so sick and have fallen so far behind, I don't even know what I have left to do. My notes are covered over in a mess of cigarette ashes and coffee stains. Duke and King sit around all day reading the papers and teasing me about my condition. They tell me I should see a doctor, that maybe he can write me a prescription and I can meet some of their other friends, but I tell them I have drawn the line with the two of them. They just look at me and laugh, knowing I can't get rid of them, and though I grow weaker every day they stay, I cannot just throw them out. It hurts too much. Meanwhile, they are looking stronger and stronger, wearing nicer and nicer clothes, and they no longer have big parties every day. They just sit around playing cards, always at the ready to bully me if I so much as ask a question. I have had the most insane arguments imaginable with them. They are irrational and never stick to any kind of logic. They know which buttons to push to drive me into a frenzy, then laugh and deal another hand. I know they are waiting for me to die, and I feel my health slipping away a bit each day. Finally I can't get out of bed. Neither one of them lifts a finger to help me. They just stand in front of the door watching me get weaker. As my eyes start to close, the sun setting through the window behind them appears to be shining through them. I suddenly remember what hope feels like. It washes over me when it appears they become transparent and actually start to disappear. I feel for a moment that I will be saved, but then I realize that they are a part of me and are dissolving before my eyes at my current rate of decline. They grimace without feeling or remorse, and would each cast a long shadow if it weren't for the fact that the sunlight is now streaming through them as if they were made of the finest, most sheer silk. It is in a great softness that they finally dissipate, and in the blinding light where they once stood, I close my eyes on my foul friends.

Crash Landing

My brother and I are the landing gear on a small plane, and we have worked in tandem for many years helping to take the craft up and bring it down safely without incident. We like to think of it as holding up something that is important, that we share a duty not just to one another but to the plane itself, that we serve it and will go down with it if anything goes wrong. So we must always be on our toes, literally, and run into the wind to offer loft to the wings, and plant our heels down on landing, not all at once, but gradually, so as to slow the plane without breaking our legs in the process.

While in flight, my brother has never just "gone along for the ride" if that makes sense. He likes to dangle, to hang by one arm and show off, to do pull-ups in the clouds and hide behind a strut so that I might think he has somehow fallen off when we emerge into clear air. It worked the first few times, and I'll never forget the panic I felt, but now I just wait for him to show himself again, come down from behind the strut with that smile on his face, or that straight face he uses, anything to get me to smile, and however it is, I do end up laughing it's all so ridiculous.

But on my side of the plane, it's just business. I hang and try to respond to what I think the pilot has in mind. I may fly flat and be parallel with the ground, or I may hang straight down if it helps to level the plane. It would work better if my brother would ever bother to assist me, but he's always too busy testing himself as in a wind tunnel, drifting this way or that, enjoying the power of the wind, gliding and soaring as if it were the first time he had ever flown. In some ways I've always admired his youthful temperament, but in other ways, everything he does on his side makes my work that much harder. I have to compensate for his throwing the plane slightly off. If I didn't, the pilot might be more quick to notice and seek to remedy the situation, replacing my brother with someone more like me, someone I don't know, and that is unacceptable to me, so I do my best to be his counterpoint, so to speak, and as he maneuvers for the sheer pleasure of it, I'm operating in a kind of measured or experienced synchroneity, and where one might think to see just your average landing gear, we would probably appear to be some daredevil acrobatic team to untrained eyes, but all this takes place only in the higher altitudes where eyes on the ground wouldn't be able to make out that anything untoward was going on.

The plane has a spotless safety record, and there has never been anything but routine maintenance where we are concerned. I have always tried to look at it that each part has its own personality and that my brother operates within design parameters, but something in my gut has always told me differently, that he's really a danger to himself and everyone around him. That must be how it is, or I wouldn't be constantly conscious of his activity as it affects the flight, always assisting, compensating, correcting, and trying to do this all surreptitiously since he is very sensitive at the mere suggestion that there is anything questionable in how he manages his side of the plane. We get along fine as long as I just let him be who he is, and I guess I'm just being me to worry about consequences and undertake the more boring but necessary tasks in our cooperation.

Over many thousands of flight hours, however, there are always going to be incidents of one kind or another, even those situations that we can do nothing about, meaning that it's totally in the pilot's hands, and we're just going along for the ride. There have been a couple of

unexpected thunderstorms where both my brother and I hung on for
dear life. There were no jokes, no smiles, no testing the force of the
wind as its power was fierce and quite effective at turning the carefree
mood into one of cowering respect. Somehow we got through those,
and we came away understanding that stress or design parameters cannot always line up with weather, with its power that can be boundless,
and knowing ignorance is the biggest enemy, we've waited in the
hanger together while storm systems passed overhead that we had no
doubt would have torn us apart had we been up there.

The worst of it happened on a take-off recently when my brother
dangled a little too far down when he should have retracted. The plane
had a full load and needed a good headwind and the full runway if it
was going to clear the trees. My brother understood this, but he was
goofing around again, showing off I guess, though I don't know who
he thinks his audience is because he certainly knows the dangers and
how I feel about it. But this time a tree interfered with his legs just as
it looked like we were going to make it, and I could see what it took
out of him instantly. There's an unmistakable look of desperation or
distress that doesn't even ask for help. It just seems to accept that fate
has turned and a kind of shock takes over. He was holding on tight,
but I could see his legs were broken, both of them, and his feet were
pretty well mangled up, so I assumed multiple breaks there. He was
useless as a landing gear, and now the pilot, knowing something had
gone wrong, was turning the plane around to attempt a landing.

I knew enough about landings and the tandem necessities of working together with my brother to realize that this was not going to
work well. My legs were fine, but as soon as we touched ground, my
brother's legs were just going to drag, and I knew I would not be able
to support the whole plane myself, not with a full load. No matter
how I might try to run and hold everything up, as soon as the craft
touched down, I would be unable to maintain a straight line, and the
plane would spin out and certainly wreck. So I really only had one
choice, which was to buckle when the impact came, and let my legs
be chewed up and broken so as to equalize and balance the landing
across the bottom of the fuselage, which I succeeded in doing at great
cost to my own performance parameters.

I had signaled my brother to pull himself up, which wouldn't totally spare him, but at least it lessened the final damage. The plane landed safely, and there were no further injuries, but we no longer fly. I still remember the way he combined soaring with smiling, and to some extent I feel that I am somehow responsible for ripping that smile from his face, that by believing in and enforcing limits on his flights, I was taking away from a spiritual innocence that was inborn, demanding that he be something he wasn't, breaking a law of nature as it were. But I couldn't stop him, and it is evident from the end result that allowing him free reign would have brought the same result, only sooner. I know he looks at me as one who must think himself superior for being more steady, more determined to obey the rules, as one who missed something for not having enjoyed life more.

It is sad that we are now on opposite sides of a barge heading down river. How slowly everything passes, but it still reminds me of flying. The slow and meandering river is nothing like the sky, but I used to watch cities pass by slowly from above. Now I watch everything slowly pass from close up, but I feel as if I am crawling. Nothing I do facilitates or alters the movement of the barge. My brother is a sullen wreck, refusing to look at me. We are coming in for the real final landing now, with only memories of what we once were together, with no ceremonial decommissioning, no band playing music, no retirement party with hors d'oeuvres. I still have reason to hope that he will look at me before we're recycled, maybe see me as another half that he needed to make it as far as he did, but ultimately we are separate, and each must face ultimate finality alone.

The Well

Ever since I can remember, I've known about the well. I've even had a bucket on a rope that turning a crank sends down, but that rope long since frayed away and left me here up top looking down. I always expect to see my face, but I don't see much of anything except the darkness of my soul and my sin.

I just carry the well around in me, and I don't have to say anything about it to anyone. As long as everything in it stays down there, I get along alright. When I was a kid, grownups used to talk about what needs to be put in the well and left down there forever. I was taught to fear what was in the well when I was born, things that were always there that I couldn't kill or stop from being there but that needed to stay down there, that it was each person's job to manage their own well, keep a lid on it as it were, but even when I was little, I knew about all the things that are down there from seeing them all up and about everywhere on the surface, right out in front of my eyes because so many people didn't have the same idea of what belongs down there and what should be allowed to crawl up from out of the well. I had these neighbors who drank too much. They might as well have been pouring their liquor into their wells for the overflow it caused. Everything in the well came gushing up when they were drinking, and they would come over and get my parents to toss back a few, and I would sit in bed thinking about their being a whole lot of well sewage flowing around just outside my door, flowing out of the wells of the very people who would warn me about how to manage my own well. They would take me to church where I heard the same things generally, about how everyone has a deep well full of bad stuff they have to maintain and contain, even a remedy for cleaning it; and though I tried my best to believe in all of that, to me it wasn't a well if it didn't have a bucket and a rope I could crank up and down. If I was going to be told I had a well inside me, how could I believe it without seeing it for myself, so I got to looking inside myself for any holes in the ground, looking where there was desire in me, or bad thoughts and such, and I guess I found the well fairly easily. My friends helped me find it sooner than I could honestly say I found it myself. There were boys in my neighborhood who were already so well versed in going down into their own wells and coming back up with all sorts of stuff that whenever I hung around with them, I was pretty sure I knew where the well was in me though I wasn't so quick to go jumping into it like they were. But in my spare time before I would go to sleep I would lie in bed thinking about things, and that's where I set up the rope and bucket system. I'd crank the bucket down, then bring it up to see what was in it. I wasn't ready to go crawling down there all by myself with all the warnings I'd gotten, even though it seemed everyone I knew, kids and grownups alike, all had an open door policy with their wells. I didn't see any shame in them, but I still knew that none of it was right what they were doing, and I knew what came from the well and what didn't.

As the years went by, I cranked that bucket down so many times like I said that the rope finally shredded. The bucket fell down there, pretty well used up and falling apart before it fell. I guess I was in my teens by then, and that's when I began to actually go down there myself. I guess I never felt good about it after I came back. It sort of stuck with me for a couple of days afterwards, but after a week of not going, I would want to do it again, and as the years passed, I got pretty good at climbing up and down into my well. I even got good at basically portraying myself as not having much to do with wells, meaning I kept a lid on it, made myself always appear to be the best I could be with everyone, and I think people generally appreciated the fact that I was able to control myself, that I did not exhibit the general characteristics of a well dweller, and there were still lots of those everywhere. It's just that being with people who are able to control this kind of thing that exists inside always felt better than cavorting around with those who made it obvious that they didn't care one way or the other.

Recently, I've started noticing that the entire emphasis in society has changed to affirm the well as opposed to condemning it. It isn't totally universal. I mean, the affirming part has to do with certain groups who are seen as being allowed to dip into their well and express the things like hate and anger, while members of other groups still have to keep their wells hidden and closed up. It's a double standard to have gushers going over there while most people over here still believe in lining up according to principle even though down deep they understand the general idea of it. It makes keeping things suppressed appear to be a bad idea on the one hand, but on the other it almost looks like they are saying that there is no well, that it's better to just let everything out, that there's no benefit, no reason for harboring anything, while at the same time we cannot release anything from our wells because we are not of the group that has the green light to gush and splash venom everywhere. We're actually still expected to stand pat, respectfully taking the acid reflux spit on us and allow it to be fully absorbed into our systems so that it can do the greatest possible damage, which is seen as necessary change and good for everyone. Privately, we are tending in groups to gush more frequently from our wells than ever, and seeing all these adults, some gushing publicly, others gushing in smaller circles, reminds me of when I was a child learning the importance of keeping my well covered and in check, all while watching and listening to the world around me, which for all intents and purposes was failing miserably at following its own precepts and advice.

I find myself doing the same thing now. I tell my children about the right things, and how important it is to be aware of their well and not letting things from down there come to the surface and infect and infest their lives. Then I catch myself riding on top of a gusher from my own well, sitting on the spew, pontificating the spew itself to others glad to drink it, and happy to share their own swill because it all has the same label, and sounds and tastes the same.

Something tells me that my children are very much like I was as a child, that they cannot help but wonder at my advice when they see a different world before them. I know my son had a stronger rope and bucket system at a younger age than I did, and his friends were worse than mine, at least it seemed so to my eyes, though I'm not sure because the well water has a way of distorting vision.

By and large, I feel that everything that belongs in the well is still known as having come from the well, but because I once believed the world was better during a time of innocence, now I tend to think the world has gotten worse than it was then. I have reason to believe the world hasn't changed so much as I am now an adult in a world where all wells are interconnected and form a kind of complex circulatory system for the entire world. The lifeblood of the world is what used to be found only in the well. I think the circulatory system of the world hasn't changed much. I believe the world of my parents was equally complicated for them, and that they realized at some point that there's a price to pay for becoming so comfortable with the wells, which is that the truth we tell our children become lies if measured by the way we live. The price we pay is a kind of slow death. We are ground away slowly into the ground, shadows of what we once were, and the warnings become even more vital and important. We find ourselves whispering to our grandchildren never to forget the dangers of the well. We tell them that when Jack and Jill went to the well for a pail of water how Jack fell down and broke his crown and Jill came tumbling after. But what we don't tell them is that someone dug the well and taps into it to supply the world with all its needs, even the need to die.

The last thing I want to do before I die is take all those things the well has done to change me and scrape them off of me like skin from bones and dump it back into the well, that if I can only go out clean as one bone, and that being from the tip of one of my pinky fingers, then let me do that, and I don't blame anyone else for what I've become because I made my own choices to explore the well and learn how to balance on its eruptions. In some ways that's the whole point of life, to be able to live with others, and since everyone lives on the contents of their own well and connects through the system of connections of all the wells in the world, one is certainly going to feel alone not to do that. But I don't tell that to my children. I tell them to resist it, to fight it, and I hope that when they have had enough or are at the end that when the scraping's done that they will have more than a tiny finger bone to show as what they managed to preserve untainted by the world. I would be surprised we don't just throw our babies down the well from the start if I didn't know that all the while we live we know the well and it's place without being told. We just can't help what we do. It's in our nature, just as it's in our nature to wish we were stronger, more capable, even perfect, and we can envision that easily, especially from the bottom of the well where we end up spending most of our time after a certain point in life.

Confessions

I find I have an awful sore on me, and it's huge and painful. I hide it under a large, loose fitting sweat shirt before going out because I feel ashamed of it. Once outside, I see similar sores on everyone, and I ask someone about them and learn they are called "confessions." I also learn that they can be removed but generally nobody does anything about them however they may impair or impede one.

I myself feel my own particular "confession" isn't helping me at all. Since I discovered it, all I've done is think about it. Even at very rare moments when I don't feel it hurting, I gently touch it to see if it is still there, which starts the pain again like an engine. Some confessions on others seem either far worse or much smaller than mine, and as much as they try to hide them, they seem obvious to me. Some are oozing and dripping over one's feet making that person slide and fall all over the place. I wonder why they wouldn't have it removed. I think I should do something about mine, but much as it seems I just discovered it, the only time I can recall not having it is when I was a child, and it seems as I survey the children in the schoolyard that they are confession free when their confessions are very small, but some have very large burdens and are carrying around these burdens which are sized according to the size of the confessions of their parents.

Some children seem just laid out flat by them, bruised but still smiling, and I can see where their big sores will start to grow. I go to a doctor who tells me he cannot remove them because they are inextricable, part of all experiences combined, tied under the skin to the heart. All I can answer is, "Take out my heart then! I don't want it!"

The Mirror

I am standing in the living room of the home where I lived as a boy and I'm looking out the window across snowy lawns watching my neighbor, a man my father's age who died some twenty or so years ago and who moved away with his family when I was very young. Somehow his movements are causing me to move in the same way, and I am mirroring him in every way. Even with my back turned toward the window as he faces my house, I can still see what he is doing in my mind's eye and continue to imitate his motions exactly.

At some point he leaves, and I find myself looking in the mirror doing the same things he did over and over again, and I see that I am a man, not a boy, and it strikes me suddenly that I actually never did any of the things my father and neighbors did over my lifetime. I never served in the military or fought in a war as they did, never sacrificed my time in service as they did, never married and had a family to which I devoted myself as they had, never just lost myself in matters of day-to-day life year after year after year, doing things like taking out the garbage, mowing the lawn, buying groceries, feeding the cat or dog, ushering in church, assisting at pancake day, coaching the kids baseball or basketball team, speaking at the school on Parents Day, handing out candy for trick or treaters, getting up early every morning and driving to work in the city. I did none of those things, and as I stand there in front of the mirror going through the motions, I can just start to feel in my chest the first cells of a heart forming in the hollowness where one had never existed before.

Coat of Rings

There is a general alarm, and an evacuation is ordered from this old building. As I look around, I know this is a place that historically was used to process people, put them through, arrange them for life in some small way whether it was to keep records or provide permits and licenses. Whatever it is that is coming, it is quite successful in getting everyone out ahead of me. They say they are going, and I know where they are headed, but I am not ready to follow, for as they open the doors to leave, such a bitter cold rushes in that I realize it is a huge threat of its own to take lives trying to evade an approaching disaster. From what I can tell, everyone leaving is quite bundled up and seems prepared for the journey. It's every man for himself though, and they are taking whatever they need to survive, leaving nothing behind that will help me. I'm not sure how I'm going to do it, but I must act immediately and use everything I have in my possession and join them quickly in this mad dash for survival.

As I get my things, it is almost like cutting through a tree and counting rings, because the things that I have before me all speak of previous times leading up to now. A tree ring will indicate it's been a good year of rain because it's wide or thick in the layout. Another ring will be thin, and you'll know it wasn't such a good year. Some of the shirts have defects in them, which I notice as I am donning them in layers, knowing this is the best way to go if I am going to survive the cold. I wonder as I am dressing, putting each one on, whether it will be enough to make it.

Donning each garment, I can instinctively feel the overall weight, and I know I am still far off from having enough around me. No matter how much I put on, I still don't have the feeling that I am going to be able to make the crossing, that I will survive. As I grab each one and unfold it to wear, I remember its story, the time when I wore it regularly, and each one tells a different tale of hardship and has the scars to prove it. One in particular is missing the whole bottom portion when a kind of fungus raged through the community. All that is left after I took the scissors to it is the top portion and one sleeve, and there is still a big hole in the back. But at least the cloth that is left is uninfected. But even though I had salvaged enough of it to slip over me back on that day, I have cut it apart to the point that there isn't much left now to help me though I must treat everything in its own way as something I'll need for my journey, so even if I can only use it to pad a pocket, that is what I must do.

As I near the end of the pile, I begin to feel cramped in my movements, and I'm also feeling the heat of wearing too many clothes. I can hardly bend my arms anymore to put anything on, and it occurs to me that I'm like a tree now, bearing each garment like a ring that speaks of a time in my life, and none of them speak very well of it, and on the whole I'm not looking very healthy and prosperous. I know from how I laid it all over me that there are some spaces where holes overlap, meaning there will be areas with less insulation than others where the pockets of double material line up.

One arm has fewer sleeves, so if I don't make it, that one will probably freeze before the other. Standing there, ready now or never to make an attempt at a future, I have become a kind of historical record of my tattered life. Even with all of it surrounding me, I still do not feel there is enough to go forward, and yet that is exactly what I must do because something else is encroaching that was forcing my expulsion through the doors, through the snow, up the hill and wherever else I am going, though counting my steps and checking the distance against the weather, I do not feel that there is enough sap in my roots to carry me through to the spring, and when I am finally ready and open the door, as I rush out, I feel the freezing wind like an axe cutting through me.

Guided Tour

I don't often grant anyone a chance to do this, but since you've managed to stay within the general periphery without assault on the exterior, I was thinking perhaps to invite you in for a view of my inner garden, something that I was also hoping you might surmise from being around me all this time, though there is some doubt whether I'm about to do the right thing to let you in. We're just going to have to wait out the current storm or assault on my domain. I'll stay with you here as long as I can, but at times I will probably need to address the bombardment and exert some energy to protect myself. I can generally do this without fighting back, with good eating and sleep, by waving off the very idea that anything warlike is happening, but I don't deny the scars I've sustained over the years.

Sometimes I feel like everywhere I step is a scar, that there is no place that hasn't been struck repeatedly and hardly given time to heal. Life is just a constant battering, and so we tend to be careful about whom we allow access. There needs to be trust and mutual understanding, for what you are about to see would be an excellent supply of ammunition if in the long run you turn out not to be a friend.

But let me say that you're in no danger by either a miss or a deflection of being hit by anything intended for me. If I form an umbrella and hide under it, you can stay where you are. Those missiles can only harm me and in no way can strike you or anything else. I have developed quite a tough skin against anything and everything they can throw at me, and they don't even know that through it all I've managed to cultivate an inner garden, that inside me there is this pristine place where I walk in peace, reflecting on the good in humanity, not making plans for retaliation. I wouldn't want any part of that.

Since we can't get in there right now, and as long as this is still a kind of trial period, a time of being one step closer as it were, I'll just go on explaining a little about what the garden is and what it means. Pardon me for the long silence there, but there was another strike. I believe it was actually an unexploded bomb, something that fell upon me recently and was timed to go off just now. Some of these things have been devised so hatefully as to explode multiple times, being of the psychological sort of warfare where an idea is planted that causes damage for a time, and whenever it is later remembered for the injuries it caused, then further damage is incurred. I believe I have been targeted by these kinds of weapons for a reason, which is that they tend to work well on me. I seem somehow to revisit the battlefield in my mind only to step on a mine so to speak, and even though I have this garden, this quiet place within myself that should keep me from reliving the horrors of yesterday, I keep stepping into them for some reason, almost as if I enjoy it.

I would argue that I do it in order to better understand the enemy, to discover some weakness, something I may have overlooked in previous forays. But sadly, I have never had success reliving a punishing event without further punishment and pain, so I have sought lately to expand the garden, and I've had so much success doing that recently that it makes me even more desirous of sharing it with others, though whenever I'm in the garden, I feel that others must sense it in me, that they must know about it, hard to believe as it may be.

But yes, it's true. It's here, and it extends so far and wide. There's so much green in it, and the grass around it is so lush that I would recommend no shoes just so you can experience the sensations on the bottom of the feet. It's just that wonderful.

But again, I need to back away here as I've received a new dispatch that brings to light a combination of my best intentions with chains and hooks lashing blindly from across the trenches. It's strange and troubling how they manage to wrap together, braid themselves into a weaving that almost makes me look like a party to the whole affair, that I have had my hand in it all the time, that I deliberately asked for the chains and hooks at specific moments, where these requests are embossed in high relief so that there is no mistaking what must be seen as my having bad intentions of inciting this confounding result every step of the way, every link in the chain tied to something I have said or done to demand a great anchor to drop into my domain in order that the ship from which it extends can drop its depth charges and deliver me in shards across the face of the deep.

The sirens are blaring now. It seems a little late considering the bombardment started a while ago. Oh, I get it. You can't hear them. I guess it's my own tinnitus or the songs from the shores calling me to destruction. Every time I hear them, I do think of hiding, of running for shelter, but there's a problem in doing that because it's a foul, rat-infested prison that waits with cloying, wet walls and a stench that runs everywhere through the darkness.

I might be safe but wouldn't see sunlight for days. It's not like the garden, and I'd rather be dodging what there is out here for that's the only way I'm going to maintain my access to it. Down there they torture it out of you until what you're throwing up is green. My only safety is within myself, and I can only talk so long before I start hearing those sirens, which I guess is my own emergency warning system cranking up.

So we'll have to take up the discussion of your viewing the garden at another time. I'm far too wasted at the moment to even visit there myself though I know it is safe. How do I know? Because I am secure. My main aspect, my entelechy, is undamaged. So the blend of fragrances of the garden are ventilating my inner skies, blowing out the noxious fumes seeking to implant the seeds of cellular destruction at the most basic level, causing me to slowly die.

I know you probably think you see the signs of it already, the fatigue in my eyes, the weathering of my skin. You've known me far too long to not recall my better days and not consider how little I currently compare to those times. But how are you doing, may I ask? I thought so. There are fewer and fewer of us really, as many as start out from the get go. And to have a great garden is unheard of in this day and age, especially when the weapons are now embedded in everything we read, everywhere we look, personally designed on a universal scale. In the old days, a single thought was enough to send a wave through the world to wake it into a righteous assembly. Now every thought we have is singled out for judgement by the unrighteous agenda whose agents are everywhere. Every day there is someone I used to know falling further into the abyss, and even their cries for help is a ploy to have me reveal myself to go down with them. There's a certain point where there's nothing one can do, where even the garden won't help. Oh, they can sense it. That's why they call. But it's from the likes of them that you ultimately must protect it. Letting anyone in to have the run of the place can ruin in days what took decades to cultivate, particularly in this environment of dodging bombs at every turn. There was another just then.

I'm sorry. I must leave you now. In just talking with you this short time I seem to have issued coordinates for the triangulators to home in on, and hell and iron are about to rain down on me from the skies. So I bid you well, and down in my garden I will prepare to go. One of these days I will take you there to see it. You still have many tests to endure, but you passed today, which in itself speaks volumes in your behalf. Should anything happen to me and you consider my whole life in a kind of expansive, understanding way, you may even see the garden unfolding before you for a moment. If that happens and you can jump on board, you should try to do so because it's a kind of a flying carpet that will quickly take off without you and fade from memory. Ride it until it comes to rest within you, and tend it there to the point that you would know that others could see it if they were of similar spirit, and you will find yourself wanting to share it, but always be careful whom you let inside. Look for balance and a willingness not just to fly but to soar as attributes of a garden visitor. Many flowers will bloom for such as these, and though you will not see them literally, they will most certainly have green thumbs and make good gardeners though their inner fields be barren. This is why you must be open in these terrible times of war to cultivate new friendships. Only in the heart does our army grow in numbers. Only in fellowship as we have here does the enemy assault lose power and become like a bad dream. At such times, a garden in the open, shared by all people, almost seems feasible again.

Black Mamba

I have just subdued a black mamba that I would estimate is at least twelve feet long. I heard some slight rustling under the floorboards and became alert like a cat, listening and waiting, ready to pounce from a dark corner where I nestled myself. It poked its head out through a hole in the ceiling, which caught me off guard because I was watching the floor, and then it started slithering down, its tail still hidden in the ceiling tiles when it was already coiling on the floor. I didn't feel any fear at that moment, and I didn't have any training to suddenly kick in unless it was having played so many hiding games at night as a child that I was somehow comfortable in the confrontation, knowing it hadn't seen me yet. By the time the tail dropped, it was a mass of poisonous sinew in the shape of a line one makes with a pen to test its ink flow, nicely rounded curves flowing into one another randomly without communicating anything. Then it started straightening out, checking out the room, slowly flowing around the floorboards going away from me.

I didn't make a move until it wound its way finally toward the corner where I was lurking, ready to strike. I don't even remember quite how I timed it, but all at once every fiber of my soul came to a laser focus, and I lashed out heel first and caught the mamba completely by surprise, stomping on it up and down brutally yet precisely in a riotous but machine-like controlled rage. It was as if I was suddenly imbued or injected with a drug that both overwhelmed my senses and enabled me to perform amazing military or martial maneuvers. By the time I was finished with the mamba, it was limp and lifeless, and I kicked it over on its back to reveal that lighter striated underside, so smooth it reflected the moonlight pouring through a far window, and I sat down, feeling exhausted as every muscle in my body had been tensed and involved since the mamba first appeared.

As I started to unwind, it occurred to me what a great victory this was and how it was going to change the mood of the entire settlement that has lived under the shadow and specter of the mamba, both terrorized and numb to its presence. Over the years it has killed many times, both people and animals, but we never have been able to mount a concerted counterattack because it would mean we would have to tear down the whole village, and even then there would be no guarantee we would find it. So we have always just gone back to the process of living, of trying to make a life, knowing that it could strike any time, hoping we would not be its next victim.

I was in the middle of thinking those thoughts when I looked down to see an empty floor; the mamba gone. I didn't think it was possible. I was sure I'd killed it though I had never actually checked it out closely. Even at that moment, I suppose there was a lingering sense of fear that it might still be able to bite me, that there might be some involuntary mechanism I would initiate by touching its head. Nor did I know how to detect the heartbeat of a snake, and because it was gone, I obviously hadn't killed it, only knocking it unconscious momentarily despite what I thought was a fatal stomping.

But it couldn't just slither away from such a beating. It would have to have sustained some internal injuries. Surely it had just crawled away to hide in a safe place where it would recover or die. I know the mamba can travel faster than ten miles per hour, but being injured would certainly slow it down, and its range must be restricted to a short distance from here, which in the short term would give us an advantage to finishing it off if we can find it.

This is where I am now, having to move quickly to make everyone aware of the fact that the mamba has been dealt a severe injury and is vulnerable. I go to the main building and sound the alarm, which brings everyone to the central hall. I explain everything that just happened and how we must act quickly, but the few doubters in the ranks believe I am exaggerating the effectiveness of my attack. Some suggest I froze and did nothing and wish to take credit for a situation that amounts to merely having chased it away, which given its speed means it is probably long gone. Others say the mamba has to be seen as part of our lives and even suggest it is a magnificent creature. A few of us go back to the scene, but they are concerned there is no blood anywhere on the floor. If I stomped on it as hard and thoroughly as I say, then why are there no signs of it? I point to where it came out of the ceiling, and after looking around show them the spot where it must have exited, but they end up leaving in agreement that there is no reason to follow up.

On the other hand, there is nothing to stop me from trying to find it, and I feel responsible for the fact that it is still alive when I could have finished it off once and for all. The settlement is made up of many large buildings, separated by wide swaths of open land, so I choose the closest buildings and begin a search. Along the way, I keep asking myself if it could have gotten this far. I don't see how it would be possible that it would have been able to leave the room where I knocked it out, so why am I not searching that building first? By the time I get back there, I can see how it could have cleared the area and made it to another building even at a slow pace. Every second that ticks away gives it more time to do anything it pleases, but the only thing that's happening is that my mind is being infected with a sense that it has the upper hand in every way, able to calculate my moves ahead of time and beat me to every punch. I run from porch to porch, stopping along the way to talk to people, to warn them that the mamba may be more prone to attack in its injured state, but they pay me no mind and leave me to my own devices, some of them adding sarcastically that they will let me know if they see a deadly snake so badly injured that it can only crawl.

As I think about the way it came out of the ceiling, the way it seemed to throw its voice, making me think it is in one place when it was in another, this creature gets more powerful in my mind even as it may be gaining strength wherever it has taken refuge. I realize it knows this whole area only too well and is familiar with every inner wall, every floorboard or attic compartment. As I run around each building in my mind's eye, I see myself looking through the eyes of the mamba. It could be anywhere, but effectively our fear and doubt puts it everywhere all at once, and there is nothing we can do but accept its presence and deal with it, which is why even a sighting or a near miss like this one does little to awaken senses that have long been numbed by the slow poisoning of its having been with us so long.

I go to the mayor who was just at the meeting in the main hall. My pounding on his door finally wakes him up, and when he opens it, he looks like he would wish to stomp me into unconsciousness. I tell him that the best recourse at this point is that we dismantle everything, just this one time, and though that may seem a desperate move and a long shot, it's actually the most logical thing to do. In short order we will reveal the culprit and remove it from our midst, after which we can quickly rebuild the settlement. He listens as I explain how we can start from where it happened and move concentrically outward, but I can see he is not really interested. Given the seriousness of the injuries, it won't be long before we find it, and the rest of the settlement will be spared. We can also start repairs on buildings declared to be clear and set up barriers against its return, ensuring the dismantling will only involve a small area at any given time, and areas designated as clear will remain so until the snake is finally caught, which will gradually shrink the search area. But the fact remains that using this method we will find the mamba more quickly such that the search will end before most buildings would ever come under the wrecking ball.

The mayor just shakes his head and tells me he is going back to bed. I do not understand this madness, this willingness to continue to allow this creature to live amongst us when we clearly have a chance to eliminate it. What I want to do is take on a few of these so-called leaders who would rather sleep than act, put them in a cell, then lead the effort to uncover the hiding place of the snake. But even the time it took me to explain my plan to the mayor has given the mamba plenty of time to move to a further location under cover of darkness. There could be tunnels leading to a network of hidden lairs, and to expose them we would have to dig everything up. It would obviously be futile if we didn't have the situation so neatly wrapped to finalize everything, and we could do it if it weren't for the numb stupidity of the people.

In time I go back to my life, and even for me, the fear of the snake begins to subside along with the sense of urgency for my plans to find it. Everyone else never left the more lazy way of doing things. It just has taken me a few weeks to take less notice of where I am walking or what time of day it is. The children run around wherever they wish, having been warned to be on watch for the mamba. The kids tend to take it more seriously that a deadly reptile is still on the loose, but at the same time they turn it into a game. They have songs and chants that revolve around it, and they tease one another by pretending to have seen it, or they throw a fake snake on someone's back to get a rise out of them. The tension is always in the air, and at least the kids know how to let off steam. The rest of us are just always numbed by it.

As for the mamba, it hasn't been seen since the incident with me, which gives me some reason to hope, but by this time, it's either dead or ready to strike again at any moment. It's been enough time for it to heal, and every day I'm expecting news that someone has been bitten in broad daylight. My children seem more afraid that it will bite them in bed, or so they whine instead of going to sleep. I think they do it to get a chance to have another glass of milk and an extra few minutes relaxing with a good book. We finally shout them to bed and just shut their bedroom doors and go back to watching the regularly scheduled tedium, which helps us to escape for a moment though always in the back of our minds we wonder when the mamba next comes out of hiding, from whose ceiling is it going to drop. Who will die next from a fatal bite? A decade ago it took my father, and a few years after that, my mother, and someday it will come again for me, and next time I may not be so lucky.

I'd still like to start another campaign to tear everything down to root out the mamba, but what good would it do? Everyone is too completely at ease and at peace in the comfort of the world we've made for ourselves. Part of life ultimately is a condition, which is that everyone must die, and the result of embracing that fact is a kind of resignation that comes on as a kind of numbness as if we have already been bitten, where we find ourselves fading fast into a fatal repose of being satisfied with the way things are, which is always ripe for change. When the mamba strikes, we feel it the most where we reach a point of believing we could shake off the tension forever if only we'd fight back, but we have a history of repeatedly missing golden opportunities to remove what's eating us. I still can't believe I got so close to it and failed. It's like I climbed up so high, got to the rarified air and had a vision of how perfect life could be, only to be snapped back to earth, having lost the chance to change the world.

I think that was the day I died, or at least the moment I resigned myself to growing old. I even think at this point if the mamba showed up I'd ask it to wait a moment, and then I'd go out and gather the mayor and everyone who scoffed at me, and I'd bring them all back where I'd then thank the mamba for waiting and let it take us all down together, which in some small way seems to me as another way of starting over, by removing the impediments to change. But what we leave to the young is already doomed to continue to fail for how we've tainted them with a childhood of songs, chants and rationalizations that have metaphorically mythologized the mamba into a worshipful beast. It's woven into their shirts and stamped in their pendants and avatars. They love death and see it as a natural force without recognizing the power of our own corruption and resignation. I did the same thing when I was their age and felt the songs on my lips would charm the snake, hold it at bay while I played. I believed I held the cover of the basket that kept the snake, which I could release whenever I pleased, and it was only years later that I realized it had always been the other way around.

I was at my best the day I faced the mamba, but I missed my chance. Now I wait like everyone else, fully expecting to feel the fangs at any time, ready to go without looking back or worrying that the process that took me will continue forever, having finally reached the point of embracing the snake, not as some kind of Godsend that saves us from ourselves, but the intruder in the garden that it is.

The End

www.ingramcontent.com/pod-product-compliance
Lightning Source LLC
Chambersburg PA
CBHW030509260626
47157CB00005B/1722